MASTER OF HER VIRTUE

MASTER OF HER VIRTUE

BY

MIRANDA LEE

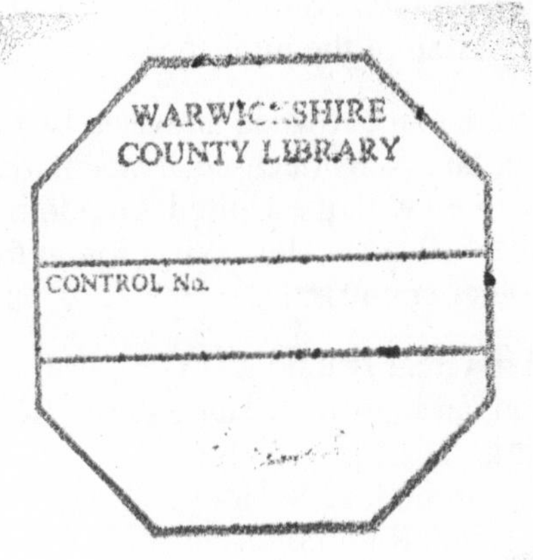

All the characters in this book have no existence outside the imagination of the author, and have no relation whatsoever to anyone bearing the same name or names. They are not even distantly inspired by any individual known or unknown to the author, and all the incidents are pure invention.

First published in Great Britain 2013
by Mills & Boon, an imprint of Harlequin (UK) Limited.
Large Print edition 2013
Harlequin (UK) Limited, Eton House,
18-24 Paradise Road, Richmond, Surrey TW9 1SR

ISBN: 978 0 263 23207 3

Harlequin (UK) policy is to use papers that are natural, renewable and recyclable products and made from wood grown in sustainable forests. The logging and manufacturing process conform to the legal environmental regulations of the country of origin.

Printed and bound in Great Britain
by CPI Antony Rowe, Chippenham, Wiltshire

CHAPTER ONE

'ALL PACKED AND ready to go, Violet?' her father called out to her from the kitchen.

'Coming,' she called back, relieved that Christmas was over for another year and she could escape back to her life in Sydney.

She'd once loved Christmas, Violet thought as she gave her bedroom one last glance. As she'd once loved this room. But that was when she'd been twelve, a whole year before puberty had struck and her carefree little girl's world had changed for ever.

Soon after that her room had become her prison. Admittedly, a pretty prison, with pink walls, pink bedspread and pink curtains, not to mention her own television and DVD player. But a prison all the same.

'Time to go, Violet,' her father said, this time from her open bedroom door. 'You don't want to miss your plane.'

Lord, no, she thought, suppressing a shudder

as she slung her carry-all over her shoulder then grabbed the handle of her small suitcase. Four days at home was more than enough. It wasn't just the memories it evoked but the endless questioning from her well-meaning family—usually around the dinner table on Christmas day after her sister's children had abandoned the grown-ups for a swim in the pool. How was her job going? Her writing? Her love life?

Oh yes, it always came back to her love life. Or lack of it.

When she'd said—as she'd said every year—that she wasn't dating anyone special right now, Gavin, her wonderfully tactful brother, had asked her if she was a lesbian. Fortunately, he'd been howled down by the others, especially her brother-in-law, Steve, who was married to her sister, Vanessa, and was the nicest man. Everyone had laughed when he'd said if Violet was a lesbian then he was gay. Most unlikely, given he was a big, brawny tiler with a wife, two children and a Harley Davidson.

The subject had been dropped after that, thank heavens. But the following day, when she and Vanessa had been alone in the kitchen clearing up after their traditional Boxing Day barbeque, her sister had given her a long sidewards glance and said quietly, 'I know you're not gay, Vi. But you're not still a virgin, are you?'

Violet had lied, of course, claiming she'd lost her virginity when she'd been at uni. Vanessa hadn't looked entirely convinced but she'd let the matter drop, for which Violet was grateful.

They'd never been all that close; had never confided in each other as some sisters did. Vanessa was eight years older and had never been on the same wavelength as Violet.

Still, it seemed incredible that anyone in her family would ever think that she would find relationships with the opposite sex easy. Years of suffering from severe cystic acne had blighted her teenage years, turning her once-happy, outgoing personality into a shy, introverted one. Going to high school had been sheer torture. It wasn't just her brother who'd called her 'pizza face'. She'd been teased and bullied to such an extent that she'd come home crying most days.

Her distressed mother had bought every product known to mankind to fix the problem but nothing had worked, often making her skin worse. The one thing her mother hadn't done was take her to a doctor, her father having insisted that she'd grow out of it. But she hadn't, not till a wonderfully wise counsellor at school had taken Violet to her own doctor a few months before her graduation.

The lady GP had been very sympathetic and knowledgeable, prescribing an antibiotic lotion, as well as putting Violet on a particular brand of the contraceptive pill which was famous for correcting the hormone imbalance causing her acne in the first place. The ugly red pimples had gradually gone away, but unfortunately by then comfort-eating and constant picking had left Violet with two equally depressing problems: scars and obesity.

No, no; that wasn't true. She hadn't been obese. But she'd definitely been overweight.

Okay, so she'd finally fixed both those problems with a healthy diet, regular work-outs and endless sessions with a miracle laser which had cost her every cent of a ten-thousand-dollar inheritance she'd fortuitously received from a great aunt who'd died around that time. But the emotional scars left behind by years of low self-esteem at a crucial time in her life could not be so easily fixed. She still lacked confidence in her appearance; still found it hard to believe that men found her attractive. The mirror told her one thing, but her mind told her another. She *had* been asked out this past year a couple of times, but she'd always said no.

In her defence, neither of the two men who'd invited her out had possessed any of the qualities which she secretly desired in a man: they hadn't been wickedly handsome, sinfully sexy or even remotely charming. One caught the same bus as she did every day and was as dull as ditch-water. The other worked in the supermarket where she shopped. Despite not being totally unattractive, he was not the kind of chap who was ever likely to make manager of the store.

Neither man had been anything like the irresistible heroes who strutted their arrogant selves through the pages of the romance novels she'd once devoured during the long, lonely hours she'd spent in her pink prison.

Her gaze flicked to the book case which still contained a large number of those romances, all of them historical, favourites that she couldn't bear to part with. She hadn't read any of them for ages, however, her reading habits having changed over the years.

At uni she'd been obliged to read Shakespeare and the classics as well as lots of modern literary works—she'd majored in English literature—leaving little time for reading romances. Any spare reading time she had had been spent reading the unpublished novels emailed to her by Henry, a literary agent whom she'd worked for as a paid reader. Most of those books had been thrillers.

Now that she was Henry's full-time assistant, Violet was also obliged to read a lot of the best sellers published around the world so that she was always up-to-date with the current market. And, whilst some of these books did have romantic elements, none were anything like the raunchy historical romances she'd once been addicted to.

Suddenly, she had the urge to see if they still held the same fascination for her that they once had; if they could still make her heart race. Dropping the handle of her case, she crossed the room to the book case where she began searching for one particular favourite, about a pirate who'd kidnapped an English noble woman then fallen in love with her, and vice versa. It was all total fantasy, of course. But Violet had loved it.

'Violet, for Pete's sake, come on,' her father said impatiently when she bent down to check the bottom shelf.

'Won't be a sec,' she replied, her gaze quickly scanning the row of books.

And there it was, dog-eared and with the pages yellowing, but the cover still as shocking as ever, with the heroine's clothes in disarray and the handsome pirate hero looming over her with lecherous intent. Wicked devil, she thought, but with a jolt of remembered pleasure.

'Just wanted something to read on the plane,' she said as she quickly shoved the book into her carry-all.

Saying goodbye to her mother was the only difficult part in leaving. Her mother always cried.

'Don't wait till next Christmas to come home, love,' her mother said, sniffling into a wadful of tissues.

'All right, Mum,' Violet said, biting her own bottom lip.

'Promise me you'll come home for Easter.'

Violet searched her mind for any excuse. But couldn't find one.

'I'll try, Mum. I promise.'

Her father didn't talk during the drive to the airport. He wasn't much of a talker. A plumber by trade, he was a good but simple man who loved his wife and his family, though it was clear to both Vanessa and Violet that Gavin was the apple of his eye. Admittedly, they were like two peas in a pod, with Gavin having become a plumber as well. Vanessa was closest to her mother, both in looks and personality, whilst Violet… Well, Violet had always been the odd one out in the family in every way.

Aside from being the only one to be plagued by acne in her teenage years, she'd looked totally different as well. Where both Vanessa and her mother were blue-eyed blondes with small bones and were less than average height, Violet was taller and curvier, with dark brown hair and eyes. Admittedly, her father and brother had dark-brown hair and eyes, but they weren't big men, both a good few inches less than six feet with lean, wiry frames.

She'd been told, when she'd once questioned her genes, that she looked like her great-aunt Mirabella, the one who'd died and left her the ten grand. Not that she'd ever met the woman. Apparently, she'd died a spinster. It suddenly occurred to Violet that maybe no man would marry her because she'd had a face covered in pimples and scars at a time when there'd been no miracle pill or miracle lasers.

But it wasn't just in looks that Violet was different from the rest of her family. Her brain was different as well. Measured with an IQ of one hundred and forty, she had a brilliant memory, as well as an analytical mind and a talent for writing—though not creative writing so much, she was beginning to suspect. She'd finally abandoned her attempt to write her first novel this past year when she hadn't been able to get past the third chapter.

Her writing ability, she'd concluded, lay more in being able to put her analytical thoughts and opinions into words which were original and thought-provoking. Her English essays in high school had been so good that her teachers had been stunned. They'd encouraged her to enter an essay competition on the subject of Jane Austen's books, first prize being a scholarship to study for an arts degree at Sydney University, where all her fees and books would be paid for.

She'd won it before she'd also noted the scholarship included two thousand dollars a semester towards her living expenses. It was not quite enough for her to live on, but she'd been fortunate to find board with a widow named Joy who'd charged her only a nominal rent provided Violet did some of the heavy cleaning and helped her with the shopping.

Another plus had been the location of Joy's terraced house. It was in Newtown, an inner-city suburb within walking distance of Sydney University. Even so, her father had still had to give her some money so that she could make ends meet. That was till she had landed the job as one of Henry's readers, after which she'd been able to survive without outside help.

Violet had quickly found she liked not being beholden to anyone for anything; had liked the feeling of being responsible for herself. As much as she still lacked confidence in her appearance, she did not lack confidence in other areas of her life.

She knew she was good at her job as well as quite a lot of other things. She'd learned to cook well, thanks to helping Joy in the kitchen. She was a good driver, again thanks to Joy, who'd lent her a car and bravely gone with her whilst she clocked up the numbers of hours driving that she needed to secure her licence. She would have bought herself a car, if she'd needed one, but Henry worked out of an apartment in the CBD and it was much easier to catch a bus than drive into the city and find parking.

Violet supposed that, if she had a social life with lots of friends dotted all over Sydney, she would definitely have to buy herself a car. But she didn't.

Occasionally, this bothered her, but she'd grown used to not having friends; grown used to her own company. Not that she stayed home alone all the time. She often went out with Joy, who was still a real live-wire, despite being seventy-five now with two arthritic hips, which gave her hell in the winter. Every Saturday night the two of them would go out for a bite to eat—usually at an Asian restaurant—before going on to see a movie.

Violet could honestly say that she was content with her life, on the whole. She wasn't unhappy or depressed, as she'd once been. It was a big plus to be able to look in the mirror each morning and not shudder with revulsion. Of course, if she were brutally honest, she did secretly wish that she could find the courage to enter the dating world and eventually do something about her virginal status. She hated to think that next Christmas would eventually come around and she'd make the same tired old excuse over her lack of a love life.

A wry smile pulled at the corners of her mouth as she thought of the book in her bag. What she needed was a wickedly sexy pirate to kidnap her and not give her time to think or to worry before he ravaged her silly.

Unfortunately, that was highly unlikely to happen in this day and age. It was an exciting thought, though.

Suddenly, Violet couldn't wait to get to the airport where she could start reading.

'Don't get out, Dad,' she said once they arrived at the departure drop-off point.

'Okay. Give us a kiss.'

Violet leant over and pecked him on the cheek. 'Bye, Dad. Keep well.'

Twelve minutes later, Violet was sitting in the departure lounge, reading the story of Captain Strongbow and his Lady Gwendaline. By the time she boarded the plane, she was halfway through the three-hundred-and-fifty-page book, having become a speed reader over the years. By the time the jet began its descent into Mascot airport, she was on the last chapter.

The story had been pretty much as she remembered—the plot packed with action, the hero thrillingly sexy, the love scenes extremely explicit and, yes, exciting. Her heart was definitely racing once more.

There was one difference, however, which she noticed on second reading: the heroine was a much stronger character than she'd originally thought. Of course, the first time round Violet had been focusing more on the hero, who was the epitome of macho attractiveness.

On second reading, however, she saw that Lady Gwendaline wasn't as dominated by the dashing but rather decadent Captain Strongbow as she'd imagined. She'd stood up to him all the way. When it was obvious he was going to have sex with her with or without her permission, her decision not to resist his advances had not been done out of fear and weakness but out of a determination to survive. She'd faced her ordeal with courage. Faced it head-on. She hadn't whined and wept. She hadn't begged. She'd lifted her chin, stripped off her clothes and done what she had to do.

That she'd found pleasure in having sex with her captor had come as a shock to Lady Gwendaline. It was blatantly obvious, though, that she had decided to go to bed with the pirate *before* she discovered what a great lover he was. There was nothing weak about Gwendaline. Nothing of the victim. She was a survivor because she was a decider. She didn't just let things happen to her. She decided, then she acted. Sometimes foolishly, but always with spirit and courage.

Violet smothered a sigh as she closed the book

then slipped it back into her bag. She wished she had that type of courage. But she didn't. She couldn't even find the courage to go out on a date. God, she was pathetic!

She was sitting there, castigating herself, when she became aware that the plane had stopped descending. It was, in fact, ascending—quite quickly. But why? Even before there was time for fear to take hold, the pilot's voice came over the intercom.

'Ladies and gentlemen,' he said, 'this is your captain speaking. We are experiencing a small technical problem with the undercarriage of the aircraft. You may have noticed that we have halted our descent. We will be returning to ten-thousand feet, where we will maintain a holding pattern till we have solved the problem. Please keep your phones and laptops turned off during this short delay. Be assured there is nothing to be alarmed about. I will keep you informed and trust we will soon be able to resume our descent.'

Unfortunately, things didn't work out as smoothly as that. Instead of shortly resuming their descent, they maintained a holding pattern for a tense twenty minutes, after which they flew out over the ocean where the captain dumped the rest of the fuel before finally coming in for an emergency landing. The passengers by then were armed with the disturbing knowledge that the undercarriage was probably not properly locked in. The wheels had come down but some light that should have come on hadn't.

Or maybe it should have gone off. Violet wasn't sure which. Her normally sharp brain had gone into panic mode when the captain had been explaining the unfortunate situation. Either way, there was a very real possibility that once they hit the tarmac the undercarriage would totally collapse and all hell would break loose.

There was a deathly silence in the cabin as they made their approach. None of the hundred-and-fifty-plus passengers were at all reassured by the captain's cool, or the fact that their runway had already been covered in fire-retardant foam, with all emergency vehicles at the ready. The reality of the matter was that they were all facing the possibility that in a minute or so everyone in that plane might die.

Violet wished, as she braced in the crash position, that she hadn't watched so many of those air crash investigation shows. They didn't inspire confidence in a positive outcome.

Survivors of plane crashes often said afterwards that their lives flashed before them during their near-death experience. Violet could honestly say that didn't quite happen to her. The only thing she could think of at that moment was that she was about to go to her grave a virgin. She had never experienced sex, or love, or passion, or anything even close.

And it was all her own fault. It was then that she made a solemn vow to herself: if she got through this alive, she would change. From now on, she would say yes when asked out, no matter who asked her.

She would make other changes too. She would stop going to an all-female gym. She would dress more fashionably; wear make-up; perfume; jewellery. She would believe what the mirror told her and not her warped mind. She would even buy a car under the positive assumption that she would definitely need one when she began socialising more. Not a boring car, either. A red two-door model!

No more 'shrinking Violet' for her. The time had come to shrug off her stultifying past and embrace a very different future.

If I have a future, came the awful thought.

Her chest tightened as the plane touched down, a silent prayer forming on her lips. The wheels skidded a little on the foam but they held. Dear Lord in heaven, they *held*! Her head shot up at the same time as lots of other heads shot up. Everyone started laughing and clapping, hugging each other and even kissing. Violet had never felt so relieved, or so happy.

She'd been given a second chance at life and, by God, she wasn't going to waste it!

CHAPTER TWO

LEO WAS SITTING on the balcony of his father's harbour-side apartment, sipping a glass of very nice red, when he heard a phone ring somewhere inside. Not his; he always kept his phone with him.

'Henry, phone!' he called out after the phone rang a few more times. Leo hadn't called his father 'Father' since he'd gone to Oxford to study law over twenty years ago. They'd always been close, the result of Leo's mother having died when Leo had been very young, and his father never having remarried.

By the time Leo had gone to university they'd been more like best friends than father and son. Henry had suggested the change and Leo had happily gone along with the idea.

He was about to get up and answer the darned phone himself when the ringing finally stopped, leaving Leo to relax with his wine and enjoy the view, which was second to none, especially on a warm summer's afternoon. The water was bluer than blue, sparkling in the sunshine and decorated with all manner of craft, from small sailing boats to ferries to five-star cruisers. In the not-too-distant foreground stood Sydney's iconic Harbour Bridge, along with the stunning-looking Opera House on its left.

When Henry had announced eight years ago that he was retiring to the land down under, Leo had been sceptical of the move lasting. His father was a Londoner born and bred, like himself.

A successful literary agent, Henry's life had always been steeped in the arts. His parents had been professors of history; his only sibling—an older sister—a potter of some note. Henry's wife had been a well-known sculptress till her untimely death—she'd been struck down with meningitis when she'd been only thirty.

Whilst never remarrying, Henry's name had been linked with many women over the years—all of them accomplished in the arts: opera singers. Ballet dancers. Painters. And, of course, writers. How could a man of his tastes possibly be happy living in Australia which, whilst not quite the cultural wasteland it had once been, was still hardly on a par with London?

Leo had been sure his father would soon become

bored. But he hadn't. Of course, he hadn't retired either. He'd set up shop in an apartment he'd bought in Sydney's CBD, working from home, quickly acquiring a stable of up-and-coming Aussie writers via a clever website which he'd had designed by a professional. His agency didn't have any partners, as he'd had in London, or even any staff at first. Henry had kept his client base small, concentrating on the thriller genre and sending most of the manuscripts out to paid readers.

One of these readers had proved to be a little goldmine—a university student named Violet who had a real knack for recognising raw talent, as well as being able to suggest the kind of revisions which could turn a promising but unpublishable manuscript into a commercial winner. Henry had quickly learnt to take Violet's opinions and advice very seriously indeed, the result of which was a succession of best-selling books whose authors now commanded top advances and royalties.

Soon, the Wolfe Literary Agency had become *the* literary agency to belong to if you were a thriller writer. And, whilst Henry wasn't interested in expanding his agency at his age, his father had had the nous to hire this Violet as his assistant once she'd graduated from university.

He'd also had the nous to buy this apartment—fully furnished—when it had come on the somewhat depressed market just over two years ago.

Leo had to admit that he was impressed with the place. He was impressed with Sydney, too. It was a glorious-looking city, with a superb climate and a wealth of things to see and do. Okay, so there weren't as many theatres and museums as London boasted, but the restaurants were top class, the shopping perfectly adequate and the beaches to die for.

Not to mention the harbour. He'd only been here a week but already he could see the attraction for people from gloomy old England. There was something uplifting in seeing a clear blue sky in which the sun shone brightly.

It had certainly uplifted him. Leo had been feeling a bit low of late, what with his last movie having been a box-office flop. Entirely his fault, of course. He should never have attempted to make a two-hour film out of a thousand-page novel which was character- rather than plot-based. Failure had been inevitable.

Still, it had been a bitter pill to swallow after producing a string of hits over the past decade. One of the reasons he'd accepted his father's invitation to spend Christmas and the New Year with him here in Sydney was to get away from the media—not to mention his so-called friends, the ones who seemed to enjoy saying that his Midas touch with movies might be on the wane. By the time he went back to England, he hoped the critics would have found someone else to slam with their poisonous reviews. For pity's sake, the movie hadn't been *that* bad!

Leo was just finishing off his glass of Shiraz when the glass door to his immediate left slid back and his father stepped out onto the huge curving balcony which fronted the entire apartment. Leo was glad to see that he'd brought the bottle with him, as well as a glass for himself.

'Well, that's a turn-up for the books,' Henry said enigmatically as he made his way past Leo's outstretched legs, sat down and filled his own glass from the bottle.

It was an irritating habit of Henry's, starting a conversation with a statement like that, then offering no explanation till questioned further. He enjoyed piquing people's curiosity. Henry called it his cliff-hanger tactic.

'What is?' Leo asked as he placed his own

now-empty glass on the circular table which separated them.

Henry refilled Leo's glass before he lifted his eyes to his son. 'That was Violet on the phone. You know? My assistant. You'll never guess what—she's actually coming to my New Year's Eve party!'

Leo appreciated Henry's surprise. He knew quite a bit about his father's assistant. He knew that Violet, whilst extremely intelligent, was also extremely antisocial. Henry said that, although not plain, she was a dreadful dresser with no sense of style and no confidence in herself as a woman. Which Henry considered a shame, since he said she had a lot to offer, if only she'd come out of her shell and make the most of herself. She didn't mind going out to lunch or coffee with Henry alone, but she never, ever accompanied him to any of his client luncheons, or accepted any of Henry's other invitations, which were many and varied.

Henry had always been a social animal, loving opening nights and parties of any kind. When he'd lived in London, his New Year's Eve parties had been legendary, the food and wine top draw, the guest lists full of fascinating people. He'd continued that tradition out here.

Violet, however, had not attended even one of Henry's New Year's Eve parties, not even when he'd moved in to this apartment, despite it overlooking the harbour and the bridge where all the guests would have an uninterrupted view of the famous fireworks which went off over Sydney Harbour each New Year's Eve at midnight. One would have thought she'd have made the effort to come just to see them. But apparently not.

According to Henry, she boarded with an elderly widow and had never had a boyfriend. Or, she hadn't since she'd started working full-time for Henry. Which didn't mean she'd never had one, Leo conceded. Hell, she'd been to university, hadn't she? Not even the plainest, dullest girls got through uni without being hit upon. And this Violet wasn't plain or dull.

Maybe she'd had a bad sexual experience at some stage which had made her anti-men.

'Did you remind her that it was fancy dress?' Leo asked. Henry had stipulated on his invitations that guests were to come dressed as a character from a movie.

'Yes. And it didn't seem to worry her.'

'Even more surprising,' was Leo's comment. Shy people tended not to like fancy dress. Maybe

Henry was wrong in his assessment of his assistant's personality. Maybe she had a secret love life. A married man, perhaps?

'I wonder what character your obviously-not-so-shrinking Violet will choose?' he said, his curiosity piqued.

Henry shrugged. 'Lord knows. Something a little more imaginative than yours, I hope.'

'Come now, Henry, you didn't honestly expect me to ponce around all night in green tights and a feathered hat?'

'But you'd make a fantastic Robin Hood, with your athletic body.'

Leo did keep himself lean and fit, but he was forty now, not twenty-five. Time for a more grown-up costume. 'I think the character I've chosen suits me better.'

'Why?' Henry said as he poured himself another glass of wine. 'Because you're a fellow womaniser?'

Leo was taken aback by his father's remark. He had never considered himself a womaniser. Possibly it looked like he was to people who didn't really know him. He did have two marriages behind him and, yes, he was rarely without an attractive young actress to grace his arm when at the many public events he was obliged to attend these days.

But what the media didn't know was that he didn't sleep with any of them. Well…not any more he didn't. He'd learned by his mistakes. The only woman Leo had sex with these days was Mandy, a fortyish divorced workaholic who ran a casting agency in London and who was the soul of discretion about their strictly sexual relationship.

Mandy liked Leo, and she liked sex. What she wouldn't like was being featured in the gossip columns of London's tabloids as Leo Wolfe's latest squeeze. She had two teenage sons at boarding school whom she adored and an ex-husband whom she detested. She didn't want to get married again. She just wanted some company in bed occasionally. They met at her Kensington town house once or twice a week when Leo was in town.

'I'm not a womaniser,' Leo denied, annoyed with his father for even thinking that he was.

'Of course you are, Leo,' Henry refuted coolly. 'It's in your blood. You're just like me. I loved your mother dearly, but I sometimes think it was a blessing that she passed away when she did. I wouldn't have stayed faithful to her. I would have made her miserable, the way you made Grace miserable,' he pronounced as he swept the wine glass to his lips.

'I was *not* unfaithful to Grace,' Leo bit out through clenched teeth. 'And I did *not* make her miserable.' Not till after he had asked her for a divorce, that was. Till then, Grace had been totally unaware of the fact that he didn't love her. And that he had never loved her—although Leo had thought he had when he had asked her to marry him. But he'd been only twenty, for pity's sake, and she'd been pregnant with his child. Lust had tricked him into believing he was in love.

The lust lasted till Liam had been born, which was when Leo had really fallen in love—with his son. He'd tried desperately to make the marriage work for the baby's sake. He'd pretended and pretended till it had nearly driven him mad. In the end, just before their ninth wedding anniversary, he'd admitted defeat and asked Grace for a divorce. He'd just started getting interested in the movie-making business and had realised he wanted to change more than just his profession. He'd never enjoyed being a lawyer, and he could no longer stand making love to a woman whom he didn't love.

He was fortunate that Grace had been nice

enough not to punish him for not loving her. She'd given him joint custody of Liam and they were still good friends today. She'd eventually found someone else to marry and seemed happy.

But Leo had never forgotten the pain in her eyes when he'd told her that he'd fallen out of love with her. He hadn't admitted that he'd never loved her, but she'd been shattered all the same. He'd vowed then and there to not ever hurt another person like that again. And he hadn't, thank heavens. Not even when he'd got divorced for a second time a few years back.

Henry returned his glass to the table before settling a sceptical gaze on his son. 'Really, Leo?' he said. 'What was the problem, then? You never did fully explain the reasons behind your first divorce. I just presumed there was another woman. After all, you were mixing with a pretty racy crowd by then.'

'There wasn't any other woman. I just didn't love Grace any more.'

'I see. I'm sorry to have misjudged you. But you could have set me straight before this. Why didn't you?'

'I just didn't like talking about it. I guess I was ashamed of myself.'

'No need to feel ashamed for being honest. So you *weren't* unfaithful; mmm, I am surprised. I presume the same doesn't hold for your second marriage?'

Leo couldn't help laughing. But there was a slightly bitter edge to his amusement.

'Unfaithfulness was certainly a large factor in that divorce,' he admitted. 'Just not mine.'

Henry frowned over the rim of his wine glass which had frozen just before reaching his lips. 'Are you saying Helene was unfaithful to *you*?'

Again, Leo had to laugh. 'Thank you for making it sound like that's impossible.'

Henry looked hard at his son and saw what he always saw: a very handsome, very successful, very charming man. Women had always found him irresistible, ever since he was a little boy.

His Aunt Victoria had adored him, making sure he didn't lack for feminine love and attention as he grew up. She'd taken responsibility for that part of his education which no father or school could provide, giving him a love of the things women loved, like movies and music.

Each year, during Leo's summer holidays from school, she'd taken him abroad, showing him the world's wonders and teaching him all there was to know about different cultures. She'd also taught him another talent: how to listen. Which was why the female sex found him so appealing. There was nothing more seductive to a woman than a man who listened to them. Of course, it did help that he'd also been blessed with great genes. Good looks did run in the family.

It seemed unbelievable to Henry that any woman would look elsewhere when she had a man like Leo in her life and in her bed.

'So, who was the silly girl sleeping with?' he asked. 'One of her leading men, I suppose?'

'All of them, it seems,' Leo admitted drily. 'Or so I found out later. I only caught her with one of them. She claimed it was only sex; that she did it to relax during a shoot. I didn't quite see it that way. Now, could we talk about something else? This wine, perhaps?'

'Do you like it?'

'It's as good as any you can buy in Europe.'

'There's nothing to compare with a South Australian Shiraz. And there's nothing to compare with Sydney Harbour on New Year's Eve.'

'Let's hope the good weather holds, then,' Leo said.

'It should. I just hope Violet doesn't do a runner at the last moment.'

'You think she might?'

Henry frowned. 'Actually, no, I don't. Which is odd in itself. She sounded different on the phone just now. More confident. No; I think she'll turn up. I just hope she doesn't come as someone boring like Jane Eyre. Or a nun.'

'Most of the movies I've seen with nuns in them aren't boring.'

'True. Violet would probably come as the nun in that old movie set during the war on an island in the Pacific. What was it, now?'

'*Heaven Knows, Mr Allison*.'

He slanted Leo an admiring glance. 'Yes, that's the one. You do know your movies, don't you?'

'I should do. It's my job. Besides, that particular movie was one of Aunt Vicky's favourites.'

'Dear Victoria,' Henry said wistfully. 'I still miss her terribly, you know.'

'So do I.' Leo's aunt had died a few years back, not long before Leo had married Helene. Perhaps, if she'd been alive, Aunt Vicky would have seen through Helen's surface beauty to the ugliness which lay beneath. She'd been an excellent judge of character.

'You know, Henry, Aunt Vicky would have loved this place.'

'Yes. I do believe she would have. Shall we have a toast to her?' Henry suggested.

Leo smiled with fond remembrance. 'Why not? To Aunt Vicky,' he said as he reached over and clinked his glass against Henry's. 'Who, if she were alive today, would definitely not come to your New Year's Eve party dressed as a nun.'

Henry chuckled. 'You'd be right there. Nothing shy and retiring about Victoria.'

They each took a deep swallow of their wine, after which both men fell silent.

Leo's thoughts returned to Henry's assistant, Violet. She sounded an intriguing sort of girl. He couldn't wait to meet her. Couldn't wait to see what she would wear to Henry's party. He wished that the party was tonight. But it wasn't; he'd have to wait two more whole days till New Year's Eve. Darn! Patience was not one of his virtues.

CHAPTER THREE

'THERE'S NO NEED for you to be nervous,' Joy said to Violet as they drew nearer to the street where Henry lived. 'You look beautiful.'

Violet knew that Joy was just saying that to make her feel better. She didn't look beautiful—she looked petrified. Which was exactly what she was, all her new-found boldness having flown out the window the moment she'd climbed into Joy's car for the drive over to Point Piper. It seemed that thinking about going to Henry's party was a lot different from actually going.

'I don't think I can do this, Joy,' she blurted out, her hands turning clammy as they twisted together in her lap.

Joy sighed, then pulled the car over to the kerb-side. But she didn't turn the small sedan around. She just switched off the engine then faced Violet with stern grey eyes.

'Do I have to remind you what happened on

that plane, Violet? And what you told me you'd decided to do from now on?'

Shame made Violet grimace. She'd been so full of resolve after her near-death experience, so determined to change. Yet here she was, skittering to a halt at the first hurdle.

'A life lived in fear, Violet, is no life at all,' Joy quoted from somewhere. 'But it's up to you. I'll take you home if that's what you really want. But you'll hate yourself in the morning.'

Violet already hated herself.

Joy reached over and touched her gently on her whitened knuckles. 'I know it must be hard for you to do this. Bad habits are very difficult to break. But you have to start somewhere. You can't hide yourself away for the rest of your life. You're no longer a teenage girl with a face full of pimples and scars. You're a lovely young woman with clear skin, beautiful eyes and a figure I would have killed for when I was your age.'

'Really?'

'God, yes. I had no bust to speak of, even in my twenties. And no hips either. But we're talking about you, dear, not me. So what's it to be? Are you going to your boss's party, or are you going to be a wishy-washy lily-livered little nincompoop and ask me to take you home?'

Violet could not help it. She laughed, her laughter breaking some of the tension which had been gathering inside her chest since she'd got dressed this evening.

'Of course,' Joy rattled on, 'if you ask me to take you home, I'm going to be very annoyed indeed. It took me ages to find that infernal costume amongst all the sentimental stuff I've kept over the years, then even longer to alter it to fit you. When Lisa played Snow White in her college review she was skinny and flat-chested like me. Look at all the work I had to do on that bodice alone, cutting it down the middle, then adding facings and putting in eyelets and laces so that we could give your very nice bustline more room.'

Violet glanced down at the bodice of her costume, startled to find that from that angle all she could see were two half-mounds of naked flesh oozing out of the top. She hadn't realised that so much of her breasts were on display. Standing up, her reflection in Joy's full-length mirror hadn't looked quite so daring. Such a sight only added to her nervous state. She wasn't used to showing off her body.

Lady Gwendaline didn't mind, however, came the unexpected thought. She flashed her cleavage around with panache, enjoying the effect it had on Captain Strongbow.

'And don't forget all the money you've spent on everything else,' Joy continued relentlessly. 'New shoes. Hair. Make-up. All wasted if you go home now.'

Strangely, it was thinking of Lady Gwendaline's boldness which made up Violet's mind more than Joy pointing out the money she'd spent on herself.

Violet scooped in a deep breath before unlocking her twisted fingers then breathing slowly out. 'All right. I'll go.'

Joy's face lit up. 'That's marvellous. I'm so proud of you.'

Violet didn't feel all that proud of herself. Not yet. Underneath, she still felt petrified. But to go back home was unthinkable now.

'If you don't mind my making a suggestion...' Joy said as she started the engine once more. 'Have a glass or two of wine when you first get there. Nothing like a bit of Dutch courage to settle the nerves.'

'All right,' Violet agreed, thinking it was a good idea.

'When you really think about it, Violet, there's nothing to be afraid of. It's just a party.'

Violet straightened her shoulders and steeled her resolve. Joy was right. It was just a party; nothing to be afraid of. It wasn't as though she was going to be left totally alone with a roomful of strangers. Henry would be there and at least one of his authors, whom Violet had met, or at least talked to over the phone.

Unfortunately, however, there would be lots of people there she *didn't* know—clever, cultured people, the kind Henry liked to socialise with. People from the artistic world. Playwrights and painters. Musicians and movie people.

'Oh my goodness, I forgot!' Violet exclaimed just as Joy pulled into the steep driveway which led down to the guest car park attached to Henry's apartment block. 'His son will be there.'

'The movie producer?'

Henry was always talking to Violet about his son and his successes, information which she had imparted to Joy.

'Yes. Leo. He came over from London to spend Christmas and New Year with his father.'

'And that's a problem?'

'No. No, I guess not. It's just that... Well, he's

rather famous, isn't he?' Not to mention very good-looking. Henry had a photo of him dressed in a tuxedo on his desk. It had been taken at an awards night when one of his movies had won best picture.

'Did his wife come with him?'

'His wife?' Violet echoed blankly.

'Isn't he married to Helene Williams? The actress?'

'He *was*. They're divorced now.'

'Keep well away from him, then,' Joy warned as she pulled up next to a flashy red sports car. 'Especially if that's his car.'

'For heaven's sake, Joy, I doubt a man like Leo Wolfe would ever be interested in someone like me. For one thing, he has to be well over forty. He has a twenty-year-old son from his first marriage.' Violet had actually met the son, Liam, when he'd been down under for a backpacking holiday earlier in the year. He'd stayed with his grandfather for a few days and had come into the office one day. A very good-looking boy. And extremely charming.

'Older men often like pretty young girls,' Joy pointed out drily. *Especially sweet, innocent ones like you*, she didn't add. But she thought it. Lord, but she hoped she'd done the right thing, encouraging Violet to doll herself up and go to this party. It had seemed the right thing at the time, with Violet wanting so desperately to throw off her hang-ups and lead a more normal life for a twenty-five-year-old girl.

It was obvious by the look of this place, however—harbour-side apartments in Point Piper cost heaps—that Violet's wealthy boss and his even wealthier son lived and mixed in circles where traditional values and morals were not necessarily adhered to. The rich and the famous lived life by their own rules. Perhaps she shouldn't have told Violet to have a drink or two.

Still, she could hardly start raising her doubts now. And she wasn't Violet's mother, after all.

But she did feel responsible for her. Violet had become more than a boarder in the years they'd lived together. She was a dear friend. But she'd be a babe in the woods in the company she'd be keeping tonight.

'I've been thinking,' Joy piped up in what she hoped was a casual-sounding voice. 'You're going to have the devil of a time getting a taxi home after midnight on New Year's Eve. What say I come back and pick you up around one o'clock?'

Violet looked taken aback by the offer. 'I couldn't ask you to do that, Joy.'

'Don't be silly. I won't be asleep; I'll be staying up to watch the fireworks, as always. I could leave straight after they're finished. I'll give you a ring once I get here. You have your phone with you, don't you?'

'Yes,' Violet said. 'In here.' And she lifted the silver clutch bag she'd bought for the occasion.

'That's settled, then. Off you go, now, before you start having second thoughts again.'

Violet opened the car door and got out, after which she bent down to give Joy a shaky smile. 'Thanks for everything, Joy.'

Joy stifled a groan as she took one last look at Violet's impressive bosom spilling out over the tightly laced bodice. 'I, er, might be a bit earlier than one o'clock,' she said hurriedly. 'It shouldn't take me too long to get from Newtown to here at that time of night.'

'Whenever you can get here will be fine. So what's the time now? I'm not wearing a watch.'

Joy glanced at the clock on the dashboard. 'Nearly eight-thirty.'

Violet frowned. The invitation had said any time after eight, but everything seemed very quiet. She would have expected the guest car park to be full by now and people to be arriving every few minutes. She knew Henry had asked around sixty people, because she herself had emailed out the invitations, of which at least fifty had RSVP'd that they were coming.

'Do you think I'm too early?'

'Maybe. Do you want to get back in the car and wait a while?'

Violet knew if she did that she might never get out again. Her stomach was beginning to churn again. 'No. No, best I go inside. Thanks again, Joy, for driving me. And for offering to pick me up.'

'No trouble.'

'Off you go, then. I'll be fine. I know the way.' She'd been to Henry's apartment a couple of times, once before he bought it and once a few months after, Henry having wanted her to see what he'd done with it. Despite the place coming fully furnished, he'd added quite a few touches of his own to counter the starkly modern decor. He'd put some turquoise and silver cushions on the white leather sofas and warmed all the white walls with some brightly coloured paintings, mostly seascapes done by local artists.

There was no doubt it was a spectacular looking apartment with a spectacular view of the harbour, but it wasn't the sort of place Violet would have felt comfortable living in. All the walls facing the harbour were glass without a single curtain or blind to provide privacy. Violet knew she would feel very exposed living there, like a fish in a glass bowl.

Not a bad setting for a New Year's Eve party, however.

Violet frowned again as she stared up at the still-empty driveway. Where *was* everyone? It did seem strange that no one had driven in since her own arrival. Maybe they were already inside. Maybe she wasn't early; maybe she was late.

There was only one way to find out, she supposed. Squaring her shoulders, she turned and made her way over to the glass-walled foyer of the building. Inside, a security guard sat behind a large curved reception desk. The design of the building was big on curves; all the glass walls facing the harbour were gently curved, as well as the balconies which fronted the entire length of each apartment.

A buzzer rang when she pushed open the door, bringing the guard's head up from whatever he was doing. Probably reading. He looked around sixty, a jovial-faced fellow with a ready smile.

'You'll be here for Mr Wolfe's party, by the look of you,' he said cheerily.

'Yes,' she said, trying not to feel foolish in her Snow White costume.

'Name, please, miss?' the guard enquired.

'What? Oh…er…Violet Green.'

His head dropped, presumably to check Henry's guest list.

When he looked up again, he was still smiling. 'You can go on up, Miss Green.'

'Thank you. Has…um…anyone else arrived yet?'

'Only the caterers, miss. You're the first guest.'

She sighed a deep sigh. 'Oh dear.'

'I'm sure it won't be long before the others get here. Mr Wolfe's parties are always very popular. Ah, look, there, didn't I tell you? There's someone else arriving now.'

Violet glanced over her shoulder just in time to see a white stretch-limousine slide down the steep driveway before being expertly manoeuvred to stop reasonably close to the foyer door. A smartly uniformed chauffeur alighted and strode round to open the back door, standing to attention as Henry the Eighth climbed out followed by one of his wives; impossible to guess which wife. One with her head still on. Whatever, the costumes were extremely elaborate and expensive, making Violet feel instantly ill at ease in her home-made outfit.

Not that it wasn't well made; it was. And very close to the picture most people had in their head of what Snow White had worn. It had an ankle-length gathered skirt made in a pale-blue silk, the same pale-blue silk used in the puffed sleeves. The fitted bodice was made in red velvet which matched the red velvet band in Violet's hair, hair which she'd had dyed black for the night and styled in a shoulder-length bob.

Her shoes were black patent pumps with small heels and diamante-encrusted bows on the front, the closest she'd been able to get to the shoes in the picture of Snow White she'd printed off the Internet. The stiff stand-up collar which wrapped around her neck and framed her face was white. The only major difference in her own costume was the laced-up front, a necessity to make the costume fit.

She'd actually felt very happy with her costume…till now.

'Is there a ladies room down here?' she quickly

asked the security guard before the swish new arrivees swept into the foyer. 'I'd like to freshen up a bit before going upstairs.' Despite Henry's apartment being number one, it was located on the first floor of the building, the ground floor taken up with the owners' car park.

'Just down that corridor, miss,' he indicated. 'Right next to the lift.'

'Oh, yes, I can see it. Thank you.'

Her hand was actually on the powder-room door when Joy's voice popped into her head.

You're not going to be a wishy-washy, lily-livered little nincompoop, are you?

Shame and anger revived her determination to have done with her silly shy self once and for all. With her bag clutched tightly in one hand, she moved on to firmly press the lift button instead. The doors opened immediately and she stepped inside.

This is New Year's Eve, Violet lectured herself as she rode the lift up to the first floor. A night for facing things head-on; a night where the past was finally put aside in favour of the future. *It's up to you, Violet, to make that future a better place. A bolder place. A place where you finally look in the mirror and see the truth. Your Snow*

White might not be the fairest in the land but you are an attractive, intelligent woman. There's no need for you to go through life alone. No need to shrink away from social situations just because they're out of your comfort zone.

Lady Gwendaline never shrank away from anything, she reminded herself. And, boy, she'd been really out of her comfort zone when she'd been kidnapped by that ruffian. *Whenever you feel your courage or your confidence waning, think of her and what she would do. Don't be shy. And, above all, don't be a wishy-washy, lily-livered little nincompoop!*

CHAPTER FOUR

'THERE'S THE DOORBELL,' Henry said to Leo. Both men were standing at the built-in bar opening a few bottles of nicely chilled champagne. 'Answer it for me, will you, Leo? I'll pop out to the kitchen and let the caterer know people are arriving.'

'Fine,' Leo agreed, depositing the champagne bottle he was holding into one of the ice buckets before heading for the front door.

His eyebrows rose when he opened it to find the most delicious looking Snow White standing there. All alone, he noted happily; no Prince Charming by her side. He also noted that her lovely big brown eyes were staring at him like he was a little green man from Mars. It occurred to Leo that perhaps she was thinking he hadn't bothered to dress up. He supposed his black dinner suit, white dress shirt and black bow-tie didn't look like a fancy dress costume.

'Good evening, Snow White,' he said with what he hoped was a suitably suave smile. 'Do come in. By the way, my name is Bond. James Bond,' he added, looking deep into her eyes.

'Oh,' she said, her prettily pale cheeks colouring with the most enchanting blush. It was then that Leo twigged who she was.

'You're Violet, aren't you? Dad's assistant.'

'Yes. Yes, I am. But how did you...?'

'Call it intuition,' he interrupted smoothly. 'I presume you know who *I* am. When I'm not being James Bond, that is.'

He was rewarded with a small, sweet smile. 'Yes. You're Henry's son, Leo, the famous movie producer.'

'Maybe not so famous after my last effort,' he replied drily. 'But let's not talk shop tonight. Or stand in the doorway.'

Her full skirt swished as she stepped inside the foyer. Leo closed the door before taking her elbow and steering her into the middle of the huge but empty living room.

'I came too early,' she said, sounding embarrassed.

'Not at all,' Leo assured her. 'Everyone else is late.'

Another small smile, but it didn't hide her tension. Henry hadn't exaggerated when he'd said she had no confidence in herself. She didn't, though Leo could not understand why. She was very attractive, and obviously highly intelligent. Henry would not have employed her as his assistant if she wasn't. Violet was a puzzle, all right.

'Henry's out in the kitchen,' he explained. 'With the caterers. Look, let's pop that bag of yours in Henry's bedroom. Unless you want to carry it with you all night.'

'No, not really,' she said, and followed him meekly into the master bedroom where he told her to put the bag on the nearest bedside table.

'Henry won't mind. You can use his bathroom too, when needs be. Save you sharing the main bathroom with the other guests,' he informed her as he led her back out into the still-empty living room. 'Henry!' he called out. 'Violet's here.'

Henry waddled out of the kitchen, his gait somewhat impaired by the pillow tied around his waist underneath his brown woollen habit. Leo watched his father do a double-take when his eyes landed on Violet.

'Good Lord!' he exclaimed as he came up to her. 'I didn't recognise you there for a moment.'

Clearly, Violet didn't usually look as good as she looked tonight. Yet Leo could see that she wasn't just all clothes, hair and make-up. She had lovely dark eyes, porcelain skin, nice cheekbones, a lush mouth and a good body. At least, the parts Leo could see were good. *Very* good. He conceded that she might not be so perfect underneath that full skirt. She might very well be pear-shaped with huge thighs and thick ankles. Impossible to tell in that get-up.

'I didn't recognise you either,' Violet replied.

Leo knew exactly what she meant. Henry had totally transformed himself from his usual trim, elegant self into a portly and rather drearily dressed Friar Tuck, even going to the length of covering his thick head of well-groomed silver hair with a brown wig which had the appropriate bald spot.

'Yes, but not for the better, I fear,' Henry said wryly. 'Lord knows what possessed me. Whereas you, my dear girl, look absolutely gorgeous.'

There it was again, that blush, at which point Leo totally abandoned his earlier theory that Violet might be having a secret affair with a married man. Mistresses didn't blush like that.

At the same time, he wasn't willing to believe she was pure as the driven snow. She was too attractive for that to be the case. Real Snow Whites did not exist in this day and age. Despite looking little more than twenty tonight, she had to be… what? Twenty-five, twenty-six, maybe? University degrees took three or four years at least, after which she'd been working for his father for about four years.

No, his first theory had to be right. She'd had a bad sexual experience at uni which had knocked her for a six and made her retreat into herself. That would certainly explain her lack of social confidence.

Poor darling, he thought, and resolved to do his best to make sure she enjoyed herself at this party. He suspected it had been a big deal for Violet to come here tonight. Maybe the lure of the fireworks had finally overridden her shyness. Though, 'shy' was not quite the word he would use when describing her. A truly shy girl would not have shown that much cleavage…

The doorbell ringing again stopped Leo from ogling Violet's exceptional breasts, bringing his eyes back up to Henry's face.

'Do you want me to answer that?' he asked his father.

'No, I'll get it. You can pour Violet a glass of that champagne I bought especially for tonight.'

'Do you like champagne?' Leo asked her as he led her over to the corner bar. 'You can have something else, if you like. Henry has a bit of everything behind here.' Leaving Violet standing next to a bar stool, he made his way behind the black, granite-topped bar which had an assortment of glasses and bottles at the ready.

'I'm not sure I've ever had real champagne,' she said, making no attempt to sit on the stool. Understandable, given the width of her skirt.

'Don't worry. You'll like it. Henry only ever buys the best.'

'Have you always called your father Henry?' she asked as he filled two crystal flutes with the chilled champagne from the ice bucket.

'Ever since I went to uni. His idea, not mine. I suspect he didn't want the women he fancied knowing he had a grown–up son.' He handed one glass over to Violet before lifting the other to his lips.

'I thought James Bond only drank dry martinis,' she said with just a hint of a smile curving her ruby red lips.

Lord, but she was a provocative package when she smiled like that. More so because she wasn't aware of her attraction.

'I have a confession to make,' he said.

'What's that?'

'I don't think I'd make a very good James Bond. I get tired even watching 007 in action. All those car chases, not to mention the fights. After which he has to make love to at least half a dozen different women, most of whom are trying to kill him.'

She laughed. Not the laughter he'd become used to with women—nothing forced or flirtatious, a natural-sounding laugh.

Leo realised at that moment just how jaded he'd become with the female company he usually kept. All the up-and-coming young actresses he met at parties and premieres who obviously saw him not as a mere man but as a step up the ladder of their careers. They fluttered their false eyelashes at him and flattered him endlessly, hanging on his every word and laughing coquettishly, even when he hadn't told a joke.

He couldn't imagine Violet acting that way. Nothing false about her, he thought, as his eyes dropped once more to the creamy mounds of flesh which were fighting to be freed from that corset-like bodice. Leo knew that, without a bra, Violet's breasts would settle into lushly natural curves, not stand up high on her chest like two huge grapefruits the way Helene's had done.

The prospect of spending this New Year's Eve party with a girl like Violet was an unexpectedly pleasant one. He'd already been curious about her, but he hadn't anticipated being this enchanted by her. Enchanted and intrigued.

The sounds of loud laughter brought his gaze over Violet's shoulder to the group of guests who'd just arrived. Leo didn't know the people beneath the costumes but felt sure their real characters matched the ones they'd chosen for the evening. Henry the Eighth and wife, along with Napoleon and Josephine. The men would be ruthless and their women little more than expensive window dressing. Leo had met their kind before.

What he hadn't met before was Violet's kind. She was like a breath of fresh air in a world filled with pollution.

'Why don't we take our drinks out into the balcony?' he suggested, eager to get her alone and find out more about her.

CHAPTER FIVE

VIOLET HESITATED, RECALLING Joy's warning that Leo Wolfe was someone to stay well away from.

But then she recalled her own remark that no way would someone like him be seriously attracted to someone like her. It was foolish of her to imagine for one moment that he might be. He was just being nice.

At the same time, she could not deny that *she* found *him* extremely attractive. In truth, she thought him the most handsome and the most charming man she'd ever met in her life. She'd never met anyone, man or woman, who was so easy to talk to. Except perhaps Henry. Charm obviously ran in the family, plus looking young for their age. Henry didn't remotely look the sixty-eight years he was. In the flesh, his son didn't look a day over thirty-five. Yet he had to be at least ten years older than that.

'We'll have to shake a leg,' Leo said as he swept up the ice bucket with his spare hand. 'If we want to get the best seat in the house for the nine o'clock fireworks display. Unless, of course, you want to stay in here and be introduced to all those would-bes if they could-bes. *Do* you?' he added, and threw a narrow-eyed glance at her.

'Lord, no!' A shiver rippled down her spine as she quaffed back a deep swallow of champagne.

His instant smile was wide and warm. 'A girl after my own heart. Come on then, Snow White. It's off to the fireworks we go we go,' he sang in a clever parody of the song the seven dwarves had sung in the Walt Disney movie.

Violet gulped some more bubbly before scurrying after his rapidly departing figure. Not that he got far, his hands being full and all the sliding glass doors being closed.

'You'll have to help me, Snow White,' Leo told her, at which she hurried forward and slid open one of the doors, careful not to spill her drink at the same time.

'Which table do you advise?' he asked once they were both outside.

There were five outdoor settings in all, spread along the very long balcony. The tables at each end were square and had four chairs around them; the other three were smaller and circular and had only two chairs positioned on each side. Violet chose to sit at the glass-topped table right in the middle, a decision which seemed to please Leo.

'An excellent choice,' he said as he deposited the ice bucket in the centre of the table and sat down opposite her. 'Just look at that view!'

In truth, the view was spectacular from anywhere along the balcony, as well as from inside. Violet had been impressed on the two occasions she'd been here before. But she'd never seen it at night, with the lights of the city as backdrop to the already beautiful harbour, not to mention the lights on the bridge, the Opera House and all the boats on the water, many more boats than was usually the case.

'I can't wait to see what it looks like when the fireworks go off,' Leo said, glancing at his watch. 'Only nine minutes to go. Now, does your champagne need a top-up yet? Yes, it certainly does.'

Violet was surprised to see that she'd already half-emptied her glass. Nerves, she supposed. Plus it *was* delicious. Very easy to drink.

'Henry tells me you've never been to one of his New Year's Eve parties before?' Leo asked once both their glasses were refilled.

'Well, no...no, I haven't.'

'Why's that?'

What to say? Hardly the truth. 'I guess I'm not much of a party person.'

Leo nodded. 'I'm getting that way myself. I used to love a good bash but that was before I turned the big four-O last year.'

'You're only forty?' Violet blurted out before she could stop herself.

Leo laughed. 'Dear me, do I look that ancient and dissipated? And there I was, imagining that I was aging rather well.'

'But you are!' Violet exclaimed, flustered and flushed with embarrassment. 'I was just thinking a moment ago that you didn't look a day over thirty-five. But then I remembered you had a twenty-year-old son and I assumed that…that…'

'That a man of my supposed intelligence would not have fathered a child before becoming an adult myself?' he finished for her with a surprisingly bitter edge in his voice. 'Unfortunately, no amount of brains can control the hormones of a twenty-year-old male, a reality of life which I have been drumming into my own twenty-year-old son. Still, things are a little different these days. Get a girl pregnant and you don't necessarily have to get married.'

'I wouldn't have thought you had to get married twenty years ago either,' she ventured, somewhat boldly for her. The effect of the champagne, perhaps?

'You're right, of course. I didn't *have* to get married. Another hormonal error on my part. I *thought* I was in love. The marriage was doomed from the start, but not a total disaster. I have a wonderful son whom I love dearly.'

He took a deep swallow from his glass, then glanced over at Violet, his expression puzzled. 'What on earth am I doing, boring you with my life story?'

'I'm not bored,' she said, her eyes meeting his. 'Not one little bit.'

He smiled and she thought again how very handsome he was.

'That's sweet of you to say so, but I'd much rather we talked about you.'

'Now, that would be really boring,' she said, and took another sip of champagne.

'I beg to differ. Henry has told me quite a bit about you already and none of that was boring.'

'Nothing bad, I hope.'

'Hardly. He's full of compliments. He did mention, however, that you don't have a boyfriend, something which I find very hard to believe. Yet here you are tonight all alone. So what's going on, Violet? Why don't you have some young man in your life? What's the *real* reason?'

Her eyes dropped from his, her embarrassment acute.

Leo reached across the small table and touched her on her wrist. It was the lightest of touches but it sent an electric charge racing up her arm and down through her body, zapping her nipples to attention and tightening her belly. Violet stiffened at the alien sensations, yet she recognised them instantly for what they were. For this was what Lady Gwendaline had felt when her pirate had touched her.

'I'm sorry, Violet,' she dimly heard him say. 'It was wrong of me to ask you such a personal question. I apologise.'

Even when his hand dropped away, there was no peace for her body. It felt like it was on fire. As her eyes lifted slowly back to his, she hoped he wouldn't be able to see the heat in them. And the hunger.

'There's no need to apologise,' she said, surprised at how calm she sounded. Thank God for the champagne. Joy was right about it giving her

Dutch courage. 'I don't have a boyfriend because of something which happened to me in the past.'

Leo nodded knowingly. 'As soon as I saw you tonight, I wondered if such was the case. It's not as though you would be short of admirers. Do you want to tell me about it? Or is it too painful a memory?'

Violet realised then just what Leo was thinking—that she'd had some nasty sexual experience or she'd had her heart broken at some stage. A week ago she might have let him keep on believing that, because it was better than revealing the ugly truth. But a lot of water had gone under the bridge during the past few days. She didn't want to lie to him. Lying was what she used to do, to herself and to others.

The fact that she was wildly attracted to the man might have changed her mind about telling him the truth *if* he'd been Australian. But he wasn't. Leo was going home to England in a few days. In reality, he was the ideal person to practise opening up to. On top of that, he was, as she'd already discovered, surprisingly easy to talk to.

'No, no,' she said. 'It's not what you're thinking. It's nothing to do with any bad experience I've had with the opposite sex.'

'What, then?'

Violet pulled a face. Where to start? 'It's a long story.' She sighed a frustrated sigh. As she'd discovered earlier tonight on the way here, *deciding* to turn over a new leaf was very different from *doing* it.

'We have all night,' Leo pointed out kindly.

Not quite, Violet thought, knowing that any minute Henry would surely come looking for his son.

But it wasn't Henry who brought an abrupt end to their private conversation. It was the nine o'clock fireworks, shattering their relatively quiet surrounds with loud bursts of noise whilst setting the night sky alight with a kaleidoscope of sparkling colour.

Immediately, all the guests who'd arrived by then rushed out onto the balcony, oohing and aahing as the spectacular display went on and on. Violet knew it was a small event compared to what would happen at midnight, but it was still pretty impressive. Impossible to talk during the ten-minute display, however. Impossible to do anything but watch. Then, once it was over, the inevitable happened. Henry found Leo and insisted he come with him to meet everyone.

Violet's heart sank when Leo stood up, but lifted again when he reached down to take her hand. 'Come along, Snow White. I need you by my side to protect me from the pack.'

Violet soon saw what he meant. Practically every woman there—even the married ones—flirted outrageously with Leo. It was an education just being by his side and watching them in action. No compliment was too over the top as Henry the Eighth's wife and Josephine fought for his attention, followed by Marilyn Monroe and Audrey Hepburn.

Even the men were doing their fair share of none-too-subtle brown-nosing, possibly because quite a lot of the guests were from the Australian movie industry: producers, directors, screen writers and actors. Henry had gone to a lot of trouble to invite people whose company he thought Leo would enjoy.

Now that she'd met Henry's son, Violet suspected he would have preferred to be anonymous, but he remained polite, at the same time not staying with one group for too long. His social skills were obvious as he mingled, spending just the right amount of time with each group before returning to the balcony and the people gathered there. Henry joined them occasionally, but not often, seemingly content to let his guests enjoy Leo's company without his interference, which was probably wise of him. Henry had a tendency to dominate conversations, in Violet's opinion.

Fortunately, very little of the chit-chat was directed her way, though when it was she thought she acquitted herself rather well. She didn't stammer, or become tongue-tied. She offered an intelligent opinion, usually to do with a particular movie. Of course, she'd been a movie watcher from way back, so she had a wide range of knowledge on that subject.

A continuous stream of champagne helped her confidence as well, as did Leo's hand in hers. She loved the feel of his fingers wrapped tightly around hers; loved the fantasy she began fashioning in her head about why he would be keeping her by his side all the time. They weren't lovers yet, she decided in her imagination. But they would be before this night was over. Once the guests went home, he would draw her with him into his bedroom where he would slowly undress her and…

'Violet?'

She blinked at the sound of his voice, then lifted her glazed eyes to his.

'Food,' he said, and nodded towards a waiter who was waiting patiently next to her with a tray of canapés, small puff pastry tarts with a pale creamy filling which looked and smelled delicious.

Violet hesitated. She was hungry, but to eat she had to let go Leo's hand since she had a glass of champagne in her other.

'No, thank you,' she said politely. All to no avail; Leo extracted his hand from hers anyway, reaching to take two canapés.

'Come now, my darling, this is not a night for silly dieting. Be a good girl and eat up.' And he popped one of the canapés into her startled mouth.

It was delicious. And so was his calling her his darling.

Logic dictated the term of endearment was just part of the protective cover she was supplying for Leo, but Violet had never been called darling by any man before, let alone a man as handsome and charismatic as Leo. It sent a thrilling buzz running right through her. How wonderful it would be to be his darling for real!

But such a thing happening was on a par with

her earlier fantasy, she conceded after a few seconds of wildly vicarious pleasure. Leo was way out of her league. But one could dream, couldn't one? And it was great fun, pretending to be his love interest for the night.

Her eyes sparkled up at him as she washed the canapé down with a mouthful of champagne.

'Thank you, darling,' she said, chuffed at how convincing she sounded. And how sophisticated. Who would have believed when she came here tonight that within a couple of hours she would have conquered her nerves so splendidly?

Joy was going to be so surprised.

Violet certainly was.

CHAPTER SIX

OH DEAR, LEO THOUGHT, not having missed the slight slurring in Violet's voice just now. If he were any judge—and he liked to think he was by the age of forty—Violet was well on the way to getting sloshed, and it was only ten-thirty. Admittedly, she'd been knocking back the champagne ever since she'd arrived. His fault, to a degree. She'd seemed awfully tense at first so he'd topped her glass up a few times in an effort to get her to relax.

Henry would not be pleased with him if he got Violet blind drunk. Not pleased at all.

Some dancing music started up just then, which was opportune. A little light exercise, along with no more bubbly for a while, was what Violet needed. Some more food as well. Henry was planning to serve a buffet supper around eleven which wasn't too far off. Leo decided to keep Violet on the move till then, by which time the effect of the alcohol would have diffused somewhat.

'Please excuse us, folks,' he said to the group of people they were currently with, 'but that's dancing music I'm hearing inside and I just love to dance.' So saying, he took the glass out of Violet's hand, depositing it on a nearby table before cupping her elbow and steering her quite forcefully inside.

'But…but… But I can't dance!' she spluttered as they arrived at the area of the living room which Leo himself had cleared for dancing earlier that day.

Leo could not believe his ears. 'What do you mean, you can't dance? All girls can dance.'

'Well, I can't,' she said, sounding half-embarrassed, half-defiant.

'In that case, it's high time you learned.'

'But no one else is dancing,' she said, her eyes registering panic as they darted around the spacious room. The guests who were inside were all sitting down, except for the group gathered around the bar.

'Then we'll be the first, won't we?' he pronounced. Leo had found that people at parties were a bit like sheep. If one couple hit the dance floor, more soon followed.

'And before you make some other pathetic excuse,' he continued sternly, 'even a moron can do the two-foot shuffle. Now, put your arms up around my neck.'

She did as ordered, though anyone would think he'd asked her to wrap herself around an electric fence by the look on her face. She also stayed standing a good foot and a half away from him, which made for an awkward lean to her upper body.

Sighing, Leo slid his arms around her waist and pulled her closer. Maybe too close, he was to realise a split second later as her full breasts pressed against the hard wall of his chest. His male hormones stirred, as did something else. Stunningly so. Leo's teeth clenched hard in his jaw as he struggled to control his wayward flesh. But it was a futile effort. Thank God her skirt had a lot of material in it or things could have been embarrassing.

Common sense still warned him to step away from her, to say he'd changed his mind about dancing. After all, he was no longer at an age when surging testosterone levels controlled his behaviour. Leo was often in the company of women far more beautiful and sexy than Violet, and he didn't feel compelled to pursue them as he once had. These days, his brain ruled his sex life, not his body.

But, as the old saying went, the spirit can be willing but the flesh is weak.

Not that Leo's flesh felt weak at that precise moment. It felt hard and strong and wickedly focused on the girl in his arms.

'Link your hands more tightly around the back of my neck,' he commanded her.

She did so and it brought their bodies even closer together.

Could she feel his erection through his suit jacket and her gathered skirt?

He doubted it, despite her eyes widening and her pale cheeks going a bright pink. Leo suspected this wasn't embarrassment he was seeing in Violet's flushed face and big, liquid eyes. This was the body language of sexual chemistry. Hers, not his.

Once again, common sense told him to look away; to pretend he hadn't noticed anything. Because nothing good could come of their physical attraction for each other. She was way too young and way too innocent for the likes of him.

But that was a large part of her appeal, wasn't it? Her youth. Her…freshness.

He would have no trouble seducing her; Leo was extremely confident in matters of the bedroom. But to do so would make him the kind of heartless womaniser his father had accused him of being. He could not, *would not*, do it. He already had one woman's broken heart on his conscience. He wasn't going to add Violet to the score.

But, by God, she was a wicked temptation. It was crazy of him to keep on holding her like this, so intoxicatingly, painfully close. But he could hardly stop now. She would think him rude.

'Take two steps to your left,' he instructed her brusquely. 'Now two to your right. Try to match the beat of the music.'

She followed his instructions perfectly, her blind obedience appealing to that part of Leo's nature which had always enjoyed the role of leader. At university he'd held positions of prestige and power. As a lawyer, he'd started his own small practice rather than work for someone else. He hated taking orders. But he loved giving them.

'Very good,' he said. 'Now, you just repeat those four steps *ad infinitum*. Or till the music stops,' he added, hoping like hell that that would be soon. Because, if it didn't, he was going to be in trouble here. Big trouble. Maybe if they talked it would distract him from what was going on south of the border.

'How about telling me that long story of yours?' he asked.

CHAPTER SEVEN

'WHAT?' VIOLET SAID, lifting somewhat dazed eyes to his.

'You were going to tell me what happened to you in the past to turn you off men.'

Violet suppressed a groan.

The last thing she wanted to do at this moment was talk. She wanted just to keep on wallowing in the experience of dancing with Leo. She loved the feel of his arms around her; loved the way their bodies were pressed against each other; loved touching the soft skin at the nape of his neck. She could have stayed that way all night, moving slowly and silently to the beat of the music.

'I…um…don't think so, Leo,' she said. 'Sometimes the past is best left in the past.'

It made Violet shudder to think she had even *contemplated* telling him she'd once had a face covered in pimples and scars. Whatever had she been thinking?

His dark brows drew together above his quite beautiful blue eyes.

'Sometimes,' he said. 'But not if it's still affecting the present. And the future. I gather from Henry that this is the first social invitation of his you've accepted since coming to work for him. Is that true?'

Violet felt quite annoyed with Henry. What right did he have to reveal details about her private and personal life? Especially unflattering ones. Leo must think she was a real weirdo.

'Yes,' she bit out. 'But I have made a New Year's resolution not to say no to any more invitations, either from Henry or anyone else.'

Leo should have been pleased to hear this. If he had Violet's best interests at heart, then he would be. Perversely, however, he did not feel at all pleased. He felt…what? Surely not jealousy? That seemed over the top. Possibly it was protectiveness which was urging him to warn her about the big bad world of dating she was about to re-enter.

After all, she wasn't exactly the most sophisticated of girls, or the most experienced. He doubted she'd had more than one lover; no doubt a randy university student who'd claimed love when all he'd really wanted from her was sex. It was a common scenario, one which most modern girls would have recovered from by now. It was testament to Violet's sensitive nature that she'd retreated into herself for so long. It was good that her broken heart had finally mended, but she still needed to be careful.

'It's not a wise idea to indiscriminately say yes to every invitation, Violet,' he told her. 'Especially if the invite comes from a good-looking guy with more money than morals. Such men cannot be trusted. Just remember that there's no such thing as a free lunch.'

Violet bristled at Leo's rather pompous-sounding advice. She was twenty-five years old, for pity's sake. Okay, so she didn't have first-hand experience at what men would say and do to get a girl into bed, but she'd read about them. And seen them on television. She knew men had different agendas from women. Their priority was sex first, love and marriage later, if ever!

Frankly, she herself wasn't on the lookout for love and marriage just yet. All she wanted during the next year was to find a nice guy to date who would take her virginity and leave her feeling good about herself. If they fell in love, then great. But if they didn't, she'd survive then move on. That was what the new year was going to be about for her. Moving on.

'I do know that, Leo,' she said with a hint of irritation in her voice. 'I'm not a total ignoramus where men are concerned.'

'I didn't say that. But please allow me to know the beast better than you do.'

Violet didn't like it that Leo had suddenly turned all 'big brother' on her. She much preferred the man who'd held her hand, called her darling, fed her canapés and insisted she dance with him. Her pleasure in the evening vanished, along with the fantasy in her head of their being lovers. If she could have gone home at that moment, she would have. Unfortunately, she was trapped till after midnight.

But there was one thing she *could* do.

Steeling herself, she stopped moving her feet and removed her arms from around Leo's neck.

'I'm sorry, Leo,' she said, 'but I need to go to the bathroom.' Which was actually true. She hadn't been all night, yet she'd drunk a considerable amount of champagne. She didn't wait for him to say anything, disengaging herself from his arms and hurrying off in the direction of the bedroom where she'd left her bag. It was there on the bedside table and Violet snatched it up before heading into the *en suite* bathroom and locking the door behind her.

Attending to nature's call took longer than usual—thank heavens she didn't have to wear skirts like Snow White's every day!—after which she washed her hands then rifled her mobile phone out of her bag.

Joy answered on the second ring. 'Violet! What's wrong? Why are you calling me at this early hour?'

'Nothing's wrong, Joy,' Violet replied, doing her best not to sound as down as she felt. 'I just thought I'd give you a call, make sure you're still awake.'

'Of course I'm still awake. And there *is* something wrong. I can hear it in your voice. What's happened to upset you? Did that movie producer guy make a pass at you?'

I wish, Violet thought with an odd lurch to her heart. It was then that she realised just how attracted she was to Leo. More than attracted—infatuated would be a better word. Which was silly of her. Even she could see that. Maybe that was why he'd suddenly gone all distant and paternal with her, because she'd betrayed her feelings somehow. Obviously the last thing he wanted was his father's assistant getting a schoolgirl crush on him. No doubt he was now regretting using her as a protective shield against the unwanted attention of other women.

'No, Joy,' she said. 'Don't be silly. He's actually a very nice man. But the rest of the crowd Henry invited… They're just not me. I'm glad I came, but quite frankly I can't wait to get out of here now. Would it be possible for you to get here by the time the fireworks finish? Say, about twenty past twelve? You could always record the fireworks and watch them later.'

'Oh Lordy, I don't give a damn about the fireworks!'

'I'm truly sorry to ask you to do this but at least you'll get to bed earlier.'

'Stop stressing. It's no trouble. See you around twelve-twenty, then.'

'I'll be outside, waiting for you.'

Violet hung up, put her phone back in her bag and just stood there, reluctant to return to the party. The confidence which had buoyed her up earlier in the evening had well and truly dissipated. She was back to being the pre-party Violet. Or was it the post-Leo Violet? He'd certainly taken all the wind out of her sails with his swift change from attentive Prince Charming to concerned father-figure.

A sharp knocking on the bathroom door almost gave her a heart attack.

'Violet!' Henry's voice boomed through the door. 'Why are you hiding in there? Get yourself out here, girl. Supper's served.'

Henry coming to find her worked out reasonably well for Violet. Always comfortable in her boss's company, she stayed by his side during supper and in the time leading up to midnight. A brilliant conversationalist and raconteur, Henry drew people to him like a magnet. It was entertaining just listening to him. Being with Henry didn't require Violet to say much, just smile and laugh at the right moments.

Not that she was happy. How could she be when out of the corner of her eye she watched a now-unattached Leo being cornered by the sexiest woman there, the blonde who'd dressed up as Marilyn Monroe? With depressing ease, she lured Leo out onto the balcony where they stood side by side at the railing, the blonde's face turned up to Leo's with an adoring look in her long-lashed cat's eyes.

Unfortunately, the glass wall meant Violet could see both of them very clearly. Once, Leo glanced over his shoulder through the glass and caught Violet's eye, but she quickly looked away before he could glimpse the misery in her. She hated to think what might happen after she'd left the party. Would the blonde stay the night with Leo? Probably. Violet wasn't as naive as everyone seemed to think.

'One minute to midnight, folks!' Henry announced, dragging Violet's mind away from Leo and back to the moment at hand. 'Everyone outside, please, with champagne in hand! Come along, Violet. Here's your glass. Shake a leg, girl.'

Violet hadn't been out on the balcony for well over an hour so she was surprised by the noise coming from the myriad boats on the harbour, as well as the surrounding houses. Music; singing; laughter; general hubbub. She stayed by Henry's side, who thankfully stopped a good way from where Leo and the blonde were standing.

It wasn't long before the countdown started to midnight, with everyone shouting out the seconds.

'Ten! Nine! Eight! Seven! Six! Five! Four! Three! Two! One! Zero!'

'Happy New Year, everyone!' Henry boomed, along with everyone else, clinking Violet's glass in a toast just as the night sky exploded.

It was impossible to look anywhere else then but at the fireworks display which surpassed the nine o'clock show, both with the sheer scale and variety of the fireworks, as well as the abundance of colours: red; orange; green; blue; gold; purple; no colour was left out, as well as combinations of colours.

Violet's favourite was the pink flowers which burst above silver showers of rain, though she also loved the red cartwheels rimmed with green. Everyone gasped when blue laser lights suddenly shot up from the arch of the bridge. The display went on and on, seemingly getting more spectacular with each passing second. Golden rain started falling from the bridge into the water below whilst more fireworks joined in from the tops of buildings in the city centre.

The noise was quite horrendous, much louder than when you watched it on television, but it was a wondrous sight, one which anyone living in Sydney should personally experience at least once in their lifetime.

It brought some much-needed gladness to her heart and renewed her New Year's resolution to turn over a new leaf where her social life was concerned. She *would* in future say yes to any invitations which came her way, which included guys asking her out on dates. Though, Leo was right; a girl had to be careful these days. Still, she had enough common sense to restrict any first dates to somewhere public. Dinner would do till she got to know her date better.

Not that she cared about dating anyone right at this moment.

Her eyes slid from the never-ending fireworks down to the part of the balcony where Leo and the blonde had been. Violet frowned. The blonde was still there, but not Leo. Where on earth had he got to?

'Happy New Year, Snow White,' came a voice just behind her, a suave James Bond voice which sent a shiver down her spin.

Violet's hand tightened on her champagne glass as she turned slowly round, determined not to do anything gauche like spill her drink or blush, or anything which would further betray her feelings for Leo. But her heart still pounded madly behind her ribs, and her stomach was suddenly as tight as a drum.

The smile she dredged up for him felt stiff and forced.

'And Happy New Year to you too,' she returned.

His eyes narrowed on her. He went to say something then clearly changed his mind.

Just then the fireworks stopped, reminding Violet that it was time to say good night. Good night and goodbye. The thought that she was unlikely to see Leo again was a serious downer. Still, she supposed she should be grateful to him for showing her that she was a normal girl with normal desires, not to mention attractive enough to be taken as a credible love interest for a man like Leo.

'Henry,' she said, and tapped her nearby boss on the arm. 'It's been a wonderful party but I have to go. Joy is probably already outside, waiting to take me home.'

'Oh, what a shame!' Henry said. 'The party's just getting started.'

She just smiled, then reached up to give him a peck on the cheek. 'There's always next year,' she said. 'Bye, Henry. Bye, Leo,' she added, turning her eyes his way. 'It was lovely meeting you.'

Which it was. He really was a nice man, just as she'd told Joy. Clearly, he wasn't lining up the blonde for a sexy sleepover, otherwise he'd still be with her.

'I'll walk out with you,' he offered.

'All right,' she agreed, unable to resist being with him for a couple more minutes.

Once again he relieved her of her champagne glass, depositing it on a nearby table before cupping her elbow and escorting her back inside. Violet gritted her teeth as he steered her across the living room towards the front door, his touch still making her feel all hot and bothered inside. They were outside in the corridor before she remembered her bag.

'Oh!' she exclaimed. 'I've forgotten my bag.'

Leo was quick to offer to get it for her and quick to do so, giving her a few invaluable moments for her to regain some much-needed composure.

'I'd rather you didn't come downstairs with me,' she said when he handed over her bag.

'Why's that?'

She shrugged, unable to think of a credible excuse. After all, what could she say—if you accompany me out to Joy's car I'll have to endure the third degree all the way home?

'All right,' he agreed. 'But before you go…'

His hands reached out to cup her shoulders, his touch gentle but his eyes glitteringly hard.

'I think I deserve a goodbye kiss, don't you?'

Violet was to think later that it was like something out of one of her historical romances. She wasn't given time to answer Leo's rather rhetorical question before he pulled her close and kissed her. Not a soft, tender kiss; a hot, hungry kiss which forced her lips apart, his tongue entwining with hers before she could do more than gasp.

But as quickly as it began it was over, Leo's expression self-deprecatory as he put her away from him then turned to push the down button for the lift.

'I'd say sorry if I was,' he said with a wry little smile. 'I've been wanting to do that all night. But not to worry, Violet. I'm not one of those men I warned you about with more money than morals. I don't seduce sweet young things like you. But perhaps it's as well I'm flying back to England in the near future, because you are one hell of a wicked temptation. I dare say I might see you again some day. But not too soon, hopefully. I think of myself as a decent man but I'm no saint.'

He whirled away from her and strode off back

down the corridor without a backward glance, leaving her staring after him in a state of shock. Just a kiss—her *first* kiss—and she would have said yes to anything he wanted. Violet trembled at the thought.

Thank heavens he had more control than she had. But even so…

Violet rode the lift down to the foyer in somewhat of a daze, her head whirling with a host of amazing thoughts. He'd wanted to kiss her all night, had he? How thrilling. How utterly, utterly thrilling!

And who knew? Like Leo said, it was possible that she *would* see him again. He was sure to come visit his father at some stage.

Oh, really? the dampening voice of reality piped up. *Like, it only took him eight years to make the trip down under this time. He might not make it for another eight years. You're dreaming, girl. You're always dreaming. Be real. Your fantasy lover is flying back to England in a couple of days and the likelihood is you'll never, ever see him again.*

Tears pricked at Violet's eyes as she made her way through the foyer and out to where Joy's car was parked in the driveway, ready to leave. Despite blinking madly and saying a bright, 'Thanks for coming' as soon as she opened the passenger door, Violet was on the immediate end of a suspicious glance.

'You *are* upset,' Joy said straight away. 'Tell me what happened.'

Violet thought about confessing all to Joy but only for a split second. Joy was a dear friend but Violet doubted she could possibly understand her feelings at this moment. She'd probably say she had a narrow escape.

'Nothing happened,' Violet denied. 'I'm just tired, Joy. I found having to make conversation with a whole lot of strangers rather stressful. I'm not used to being a social butterfly. Still, actually seeing the fireworks live made it worth the effort.'

'Were they better than last year?' Joy asked as she started the engine and drove slowly up the steep driveway.

'Yes. They were.'

'We'll watch them together when we get home. And have a nice mug of hot chocolate.'

Violet cringed inside. She didn't want to see the fireworks again, or have a nice mug of hot chocolate. She just wanted to crawl into bed and have a good cry.

'Oh, I forgot,' Joy said, throwing Violet a breezy smile. 'Happy New Year, love.'

'You too,' Violet returned, her heart lurching a little as she recalled how Leo had said those same words only a few minutes earlier.

'I'll bet you're proud of yourself for going to that party now.'

'I guess so.'

'You *guess* so! I think it was very brave of you, and a great start to your New Year's resolutions. Now all you have to do is buy a whole new wardrobe, keep up with the new hair and make-up and blokes will be lining up to ask you out. Oh, and start going to a unisex gym. No more of that girls-only place. You're never going to find a boyfriend there!'

Violet smothered a sigh. 'You could be right, Joy.'

'I am right. You listen to me and you'll be a woman of the world before you can say Jack Robinson.'

'And what constitutes a woman of the world?' she asked wearily.

'You know full well what I'm talking about, Violet Green. You're the one who said your main aim was to get rid of your virginity before next Christmas.'

'True.'

'Difficult to do that without a man.'

'True again,' Violet said, her mind filling with the image of one man in particular.

'With all the after-Christmas sales on, this is the perfect time to buy new clothes,' Joy rattled on.

Violet wished Joy would stop talking. She felt very tired and rather headachy. She really had drunk a lot of champagne. She was going to have a terrible hangover in the morning.

As for shopping for a new wardrobe.... Violet wasn't sure about getting herself a new wardrobe any more. Neither did she feel all that enthusiastic about any of her other New Year's resolutions. Suddenly, none of them seemed to have any point.

Because she didn't want to get just any old boyfriend. Meeting Leo had somehow spoiled her for that idea. Neither did she want to lose her virginity just for the sake of it. If and when she had sex, she wanted it to be with someone special; someone dashing, handsome and charming; someone who put her at ease and made her feel incredibly attractive; someone who'd called her a wicked temptation and had kissed her with the kind of passion which, yes, had made her want to do anything he asked.

In short, when and if she had sex, she wanted it to be with Leo Wolfe.

But that wasn't going to happen, was it?

Only a miracle would make that dream come true, and Violet didn't believe in miracles.

CHAPTER EIGHT

A SOMEWHAT DEPRESSED Violet was having breakfast two mornings later when her mobile phone rang.

It was Henry calling, she noted, a jolt of adrenaline immediately charging through her sluggish veins. For a split second she hoped he was ringing her with another invitation—a farewell dinner for Leo, perhaps?—but she suspected it was nothing of the kind. No doubt it was just some query to do with work. Henry never actually stopped working, not even during their Christmas break.

'Good morning, Henry,' she answered, pleased at how coolly professional she sounded. 'Great party the other night. So, what's up? Someone send you a book you actually like for a change?'

'No, no. Nothing to do with work. I have this small problem which I'm hoping you can help me with. The thing is, sweetie, tonight is Leo's last night here and I've organised a night out on the town for just the two of us. Dinner at a nice restaurant at Darling Harbour, followed by a show. They've brought back *Priscilla, Queen of the Desert* for a short season. It's playing at the Lyric, the theatre in the Star. You know where I mean, don't you?'

'Yes, Henry, I do know the Star.' One could hardly live in Sydney and not know of the city's one and only casino. Not that Violet had actually been there. But she knew it was a glam place, even more so since undergoing a major refurbishment not that long ago.

'Been there, have you?'

'Actually, no, I haven't, Henry.'

'Have you seen *Priscilla*?'

'Only the movie, not the musical.'

'That's good. Then you'll really enjoy going with Leo tonight in my place.'

'What?' Violet hadn't meant to sound so sharp. Her reaction was shock, not reluctance to go.

'Is there a problem with that?' Henry said. 'I thought you wouldn't mind. After all, you and Leo got along famously the other night.'

'Well, yes, yes, we did,' Violet admitted, still trying to get her head around the situation. 'So, why can't *you* go?'

Henry sighed. 'Must have eaten something bad

yesterday. Either that or I've caught a nasty stomach bug. Anyway, I still feel ghastly this morning. I couldn't possibly go out tonight. So, how about it, Violet? It's not too much to ask, surely?'

'Does Leo know you've asked me?' Violet choked out.

'Well, no, actually. Not yet. He's out doing his morning row on the harbour. The man's obsessive about his daily exercise regime. Makes me tired just watching him. But I know he won't mind. He thinks you're terrific.'

Violet tried to speak but her mouth had gone bone-dry. For the past thirty-six hours she'd thought of nothing else but Leo Wolfe, his kiss and what he'd said to her afterwards. The thought of going to dinner and a show with him tonight was the stuff dreams were made of. Dreams *and* miracles. Was fate being kind to her here, or cruel?

'I'm surprised at you, Violet,' Henry ground out before she could agree. Which of course she was going to do, once she got some moisture in her mouth. 'Leo might have the reputation for being a ladies' man but, I assure you, you are perfectly safe in his hands. My son is a true gentleman.

'What's that? Yes, Leo, I'm talking about you, believe it or not. It's Violet on the phone. I've just asked her to go out with you tonight instead of yours truly because I'm simply not up to it. Anyway, the infernal girl is umming and aahing like you're some kind of sexual predator about to pounce. Here, you talk to her.'

She swallowed as she waited for Leo's voice to come down the line.

'You don't have to go, you know, Violet,' were his first words, delivered in a rather irritated tone. 'No one's forcing you. You can always say no.'

'But I can't!' she blurted out. 'I mean…that's one of my New Year's resolutions—not to say no to social invitations.'

'I thought I warned you to use your common sense in that regard.'

Common sense! Was he insane? Her reactions and responses to him had nothing to do with common sense. She was desperate to go out with him tonight. Desperate to see him again, even if it was just to talk to him.

'Henry assured me you were a true gentleman,' she pointed out, worried that *he* was looking for some excuse to call the whole thing off.

Leo's laugh carried a disturbingly amused tone. 'That was possibly foolish of Henry.'

'Are you saying you lied to me last night? That you really *are* a callous seducer of women?'

'A callous seducer? No, no, I'm not that.'

'I didn't think so.' Was she vaguely disappointed that he wasn't?

'In that case, why the hesitation?' he asked.

'Henry got it wrong,' she said hurriedly. 'I wasn't hesitant, just startled. I would like to go with you tonight. Truly, I would.'

The sudden silence down the line was unnerving. Had her desperation shown through?

Did he sigh? She was sure she heard him sigh.

'What time would you like me to pick you up?' he said at last.

Now it was Violet who sighed—with relief.

'You don't have to do that,' she offered. 'You might get lost. I could take a taxi to the restaurant and meet you there.'

'Absolutely not. That's not how I do things, Violet. I always pick up my date and deliver her home afterwards.'

His date: he'd called her his *date*. Violet had never had a date before. This was her first. And it was with Leo Wolfe. And, whilst a first date wasn't quite as fanciful as having him as her first lover, it was still going to be a momentous occasion for her.

'There's a navigation system in the car I hired,' he went on, 'so I'll have no trouble finding you. I gather Henry has your address?'

'Well, yes, but—'

'So how long would it take to get from here to your place?' he interrupted.

'That depends on the time of day. During peak-hour it can take ages. You've no idea how busy it gets.'

'Violet, I live in London. Your peak-hour traffic is bad but I'm used to much worse.'

Violet didn't want him coming to pick her up, didn't want Joy seeing him and thinking all kinds of things. As much as it was sweet of Leo to offer to pick her up, she just knew it wasn't a good idea.

'But coming here first is out of your way,' she argued. 'Look, how about we compromise on this? I'll take a taxi to the restaurant and you can drive me home after the show. By then the traffic won't be nearly as bad.' *And Joy will be sound asleep.* 'Okay?' she added with crossed fingers.

'I can live with that.'

'Great. So, what's the name of this restaurant?'

'I'm not sure. Something Italian. I'll have to ring you back with the details.'

The sound of Joy's bedroom door opening brought a moment of panic. 'Er, no, don't bother to ring back. Just send me a text.'

'Fine. See you tonight, then,' Leo added and hung up.

'Did I hear you on the phone just now?' Joy said as she entered the kitchen and headed for the kettle.

'Yes, Henry rang,' Violet replied, not untruthfully. 'Tonight's his son's last night in Sydney and he was planning to take him out to dinner and a show. Anyway, Henry's not well so he's asked me to go with Leo in his place.'

Joy's head swung round, her eyebrows raised. 'Really? And what did you say? I hope you agreed,' she finished up with a stern glare.

Violet was initially taken aback by Joy's attitude. But, once she thought about it, she supposed there was no reason for her friend to raise objections. After all, Joy knew nothing of Violet's wild infatuation, or the passionate kiss Leo had given her the night of the party. According to Violet's report, Leo was a very nice man. It was as well, though, that she'd organised for Leo not to pick her up. One look at the man in the flesh and Joy might not have been so approving.

'Well, yes, I did,' she admitted. 'I couldn't very well say no, could I? It would have gone against my New Year's resolution.'

Joy nodded. 'True. Though I'm still a bit surprised. You haven't exactly been at your bubbly best since Henry's party. I thought perhaps you might have been going back into your shell.'

'I've just been tired, Joy. And somewhat hungover. I drank way too much champagne that night. I feel much better this morning. But I'm going to have to get myself up and out to the shops ASAP. I'll need something decent to wear tonight.' *Or possibly indecent*, came the unexpectedly wicked thought. Something which showed off her figure. And her breasts. Leo had certainly looked at her breasts the other night.

'You're dead right there, girl,' Joy said drily. 'There's nothing in your wardrobe which would do for dinner and a show.'

'Exactly what I was thinking,' Violet said.

'You'd better get moving, then. I'd come with you if my arthritis wasn't playing up this morning. But if you want a suggestion then get something black. With your pale skin and new black hair, a little black dress would look great. And, please, buy something in your size, not one or two sizes bigger. You have a gorgeous figure and it's high time you showed it off!'

CHAPTER NINE

THE ITALIAN RESTAURANT Henry had booked had an *al fresco* area which overlooked the marina at Darling Harbour. It also had a splendid view of the Star, which was located on the opposite side of the small harbour and was as big, bright and glitzy as casinos tended to be.

Leo had left his car there with the parking valet then walked over to the restaurant via a small connecting bridge. He'd arrived several minutes earlier than six o'clock, which he'd told Violet in his text, giving him time to sit, sip some mineral water and compose himself before she arrived.

By then, Leo was in need of some serious composure. It had been foolish of him to agree to take Violet out tonight instead of his father. More than foolish; downright disturbing. All day he'd been besieged by the kind of sexual demons which he'd thought were well behind him. He was forty years old, for pity's sake, not some horny, hormone-driven teenager!

No amount of logical lecturing, however, could overcome the thoughts which kept entering his head and torturing his body. Fortunately, his claim to Violet that he wasn't a callous seducer—especially of young girls like her—was still true. Leo knew he would not act upon the wickedly exciting temptation to do just that. But that didn't mean he wasn't intrigued by the idea. Intrigued and aroused.

It was going to be a long and difficult night.

Leo sighed, then took another sip of the chilled water, his eyes drifting over the rim of the glass to the people wandering across the nearby bridge, most of them coming in his direction.

His gaze was drawn to a young, good-looking couple who were walking hand in hand, their frequent glances at each other so full of love that it was almost painful to watch them. It came to Leo then that he'd never been in love like that. In lust, yes, several times. But never truly in love. And now… Now he was probably too old to embrace that kind of love. Too old and way too cynical.

His eyes swung from the besotted couple to the girl walking behind them who was wearing a short black dress which showed off a shapely figure and simply smashing legs. It was the legs he saw first, of course. Leo had always been a leg man. He liked slender ankles, shapely calves and non-knobbly knees, all of which this girl possessed.

It wasn't till his eyes lifted to her face that he realised it was Violet whose legs he'd been ogling, Violet whose legs he'd wondered about the other night, who clearly hadn't been behind the door when Mother Nature had given out great legs.

Leo smothered a groan as that part of him which he'd been doing his best to subdue all day went back into overdrive. This wasn't going to be a long and difficult night, he accepted ruefully—it was going to be sheer bloody murder!

As she approached the end of the walkway, her head turned to the left and their eyes met across the twenty metres or so which separated them. Leo smiled a polite smile and she smiled back. A sweet smile, he thought. A sweet, innocent smile. If only she knew what had been going on in his head, and what was even now going on underneath the serviette in his lap.

Perhaps she had some idea for, despite her earlier smile, she looked nervous as she was shown to his table. Nervous but absolutely gorgeous in the little black dress she was almost wearing. Not only was the hemline boldly short, the V neckline was provocatively low, giving him another eyeful of her amazingly lush breasts.

Her dark hair was done in a more sophisticated style than the other night's bob, with a few sexy strands kissing her cheeks. She smelt gorgeous too, a tantalisingly musky perfume emanating from her skin as she sat down in the chair opposite.

'Sorry I'm a little late,' she said somewhat breathlessly. 'The traffic was simply dreadful. How did you manage to get here so early?'

'I heeded your warning and left extra early. But you're hardly late. Only a minute or two. So, what would you like to drink?' he asked, aware that the waiter was hovering.

'Not champagne,' she replied rather quickly. 'Just a glass of wine, perhaps. White. Not too sweet.'

'Bring us a bottle of your best Sauvignon Blanc,' Leo ordered the waiter. 'I'll leave the choice up to you.'

Violet frowned when the waiter hurried away, looking rather pleased. 'You do realise he'll bring you the most expensive bottle in their cellar?'

Leo hid his amusement behind a poker face

but, truly, she was unique. Didn't she know how wealthy he was? Most women would have made it their business to know, or to find out. There again, she wasn't anything like most women. Of course, she wasn't really a woman. Just a girl, a young, naive girl whom he wanted to take to bed more than any girl he'd ever met.

'I hope so,' he said. 'Because the most expensive wine is usually the best. You only get what you pay for, you know, Violet.'

'I wouldn't know,' she refuted. 'Joy and I only ever drink the house wine when we go out to dinner.'

Leo mulled over this statement. It sounded like the only outings she had was with her elderly landlady. If that were true, then it was a sad state of affairs. He wondered again about what had happened in Violet's past to turn her off men and dating. Till now, that was. Since he was destined to spend the evening with her anyway, Leo decided it was the perfect time to find out.

'You have no excuse this time, Violet,' he began, using Henry's technique of teasing rather than revealing.

Her long black eyelashes fluttered as she blinked in confusion. 'No excuse for what?'

'For not telling me what happened to you in the past to turn you off the opposite sex. After all, we have close to two hours before the show starts. More than enough time, no matter how long your story is.'

She frowned again, clearly not happy with his probing her past. But Leo was not going to let the matter go, his curiosity was even more piqued this time.

'Come now, Violet,' he said in his most persuasive voice, that same voice which he used to positive effect on the people he wanted to invest in his film projects. 'You can't honestly expect me to fly back to England tomorrow still ignorant about why you've gone this long without a boyfriend? Just look at you tonight. You're absolutely gorgeous. It simply doesn't make sense.'

She flushed, gnawing at her bottom lip as she looked away and down. When she finally glanced back up at him, her eyes were still unhappy.

Now he wasn't curious so much as concerned. She'd denied being attacked. But something seriously bad must have happened to her at some stage, something which she hated talking about.

Suddenly, Leo felt guilty for having pushed the issue. 'You don't have to tell me if you really don't want to. But sometimes it's good to talk about things,' he added gently. 'Women tell me I'm a good listener.'

The waiter came with the wine just then. Leo was impatient as he went through the tasting routine before approving the wine which was, indeed, very good. From Western Australia, he noted.

'Perhaps we should order our meals,' he said to the waiter, again somewhat impatiently. 'We're going to a show which starts at eight and don't want to hurry our food.'

The waiter handed them menus, after which he explained the chef's specials for the night. Violet said that she didn't want an entree, preferring to have a main and dessert. Leo didn't care, so he said he'd do the same.

Violet was thankfully quick to decide on her meal—salt-and-pepper calamari. Leo ordered the same, along with a plate of herbed bread. The waiter took off at some speed, perhaps seeing a good tip if he gave them excellent service.

'Try the wine,' Leo said once they were alone. 'Tell me what you think of it.' Despite still dying to know what had happened to Violet, he'd decided to back off for a short while, to give her time to relax.

Violet lifted the glass to her lips and took a small sip.

'It's…very nice,' she said, then took another sip, her eyes meeting his across the table.

They were lovely eyes, dark, velvety and soft. The sort of eyes a man could drown in whilst making love to her.

After another sip, she lowered the glass back to the table, her eyes never leaving his. 'I never said I was turned off the opposite sex.'

Her unexpected statement was both intriguing and perplexing. 'Then what *was* the problem?'

She stared at him for a long moment then sighed. 'I have to go back a long way. To just before I turned thirteen.'

'Fine,' Leo said, adding, 'go on,' when she hesitated again.

'The thing is…when I went into puberty, I developed the most dreadful case of cystic acne.'

Leo could not contain his surprise. 'But you have such beautiful skin now!' he exclaimed. In truth, her complexion was one of her best features. Not only clear but porcelain-like.

'Yes, well, that wasn't always the case, believe me,' Violet said ruefully. 'All the years I was in high school, I looked truly appalling. You've no idea how much I hated going to school.'

Leo's heart went out to Violet as she told him haltingly of the bullying she'd endured because of her bad skin and what she'd done to cope, explaining about her pink prison and the books which had sustained her soul, even when it had been close to disintegration.

Witnessing her distress just at recalling those times made Leo realise how lucky he'd been to go through his teenage years without any such problems. Not only had Violet had to tolerate years of very nasty pimples but she'd also been left with scars, not just to her face but to her self-esteem. Which was why she'd turned to food for comfort, adding the extra physical problem of being overweight.

Leo understood full well how being even a little overweight affected a female's confidence. Being in the show-business world had made him more sensitive to the plight of the modern woman where her weight was concerned. He personally didn't mind girls with a few added pounds, but society in the twenty-first century dictated that thin was in.

He could see that Violet would have felt terrible whenever she'd looked at herself in the mirror.

No wonder she'd stayed at home in her room all the time. She would not have felt like going out to friends' houses or parties, even if she'd been invited. Which she obviously hadn't been. She hadn't even gone to her own graduation ball, pretending that she was ill and couldn't go.

Just as well she'd been able to escape into the fantasy world of those historical romances she loved to read or she might have done something really silly. And just as well that that counsellor had taken her to the right doctor and that great-aunt of hers had left her some money. As it was, she'd still lost the best years of her life. High school should have been fun, not torture.

'But surely things got better once you went to uni?' he said after she finished telling him about her school years.

'Not much, I'm afraid. My skin was improving but I was still overweight. My self-esteem was zilch, as was my confidence in social situations. I didn't have a clue how to dress or how to act. Being around the other students terrified me. The boys, especially. I still felt ugly, even when the mirror told me I wasn't. It was safer to just keep to myself.'

Leo shook his head from side to side. 'That's so sad, Violet.'

Violet sighed. 'Looking back, I can see it was mostly my own silly fault. It was easier to hide away in my shell than make an effort to change. Even when I lost weight and went to work for Henry, I clung to my introverted, anti-social attitude. Which answers your question about why I don't have a boyfriend—why I've *never* had a boyfriend,' she added, her eyes falling away from his.

Leo took a second or two to realise that Violet's never having had a boyfriend meant she'd never had sex. Suddenly, his wayward flesh, which had calmed somewhat during her sorry tale, stirred again with a vengeance. How perverse, Leo thought, that her being a virgin would excite him so much. It should have dampened his desires. Instead, it made them even darker. And stronger.

Thankfully, their mains arrived just at that moment, giving Leo some quiet time to get it together. Violet looked grateful as well. Clearly, she'd found telling her story extremely stressful, her face was still flushed with an embarrassed heat.

Despite feeling great sympathy for her, it wasn't

long before Leo wanted to hear more. There were still some intriguing questions that he wanted answered. After taking a few mouthfuls of the calamari—which was as excellent as the wine—he put down his fork and looked across the table at her.

'So what happened to make you decide to change your attitude this year?' he asked. 'I mean…why *now*? After all, from what you've told me, your skin was fixed by the time you finished your degree. And you're certainly no longer overweight. I wouldn't mind betting you've been asked out plenty of times.'

Violet also put down her fork, her pink cheeks having finally cooled. 'Actually, no, I haven't. I've only been asked out twice in my life,' she admitted in that charmingly ingenuous way which he found so refreshing. 'And only by two extremely dull men. Of course, I don't usually look like I look tonight. Or how I looked the other night, for that matter.'

That rang true. Henry had been most surprised by Violet's appearance. 'You still haven't answered my question,' Leo persisted. 'Why *now*, Violet? What happened recently to make you decide to throw off the shackles of the past and embrace a brand new you?'

She smiled another of those soft, sweet smiles. 'You do have a way with words, don't you? You should have been a writer, not a producer.'

'Stop trying to change the subject.'

'Our food will get cold if I answer your question properly.'

Leo pulled a face. 'You mean it's a long story too?'

'Sort of.'

He sighed. 'Very well. We'll eat first and talk later. But don't think you can wriggle off the hook, madam. I aim to get the truth out of you—the whole truth and nothing but the truth!'

CHAPTER TEN

SO HELP ME GOD, Violet finished up in her mind.

She could not believe how much she'd already told Leo. She'd come here tonight, full of the adrenaline rush which came from knowing she'd never looked better or sexier. Joy had been right; black did suit her. Violet had been bubbling with excitement during the taxi ride here, eager to see that look in Leo's eyes again, the one which said how attractive he found her. Attractive and desirable.

But he hadn't looked at her like that. Okay, so he *had* complimented her on her appearance, but only in the way a friend would have said it. A friend or, even more depressingly, a father. Obviously, she wasn't such a wicked temptation after all!

Was it her disappointment in his lack of sexual interest tonight which had prompted her to tell him about her background?

Possibly. That, and the fact that he *was* so darned

easy to talk to. Clearly, Leo had been taken aback by the revelation that she'd suffered from acne, but very understanding and wonderfully kind with his words of sympathy. Which was perhaps why she'd revealed much more than the bare details of her teenage years. She'd even told him about her addiction to historical romances!

So why was she worried now about telling him the rest? What difference would it make if he knew about her life-changing experience on that plane? Or that he would realise, once she told him the full list of her New Year's resolutions, that she was still a virgin? In truth, he must have already come to that conclusion. So, really, there was no reason to be nervous about telling him this last bit of her story.

Nevertheless, Violet reached for her wineglass several times as she went about finishing her meal. At last all the calamari was gone, along with a couple of slices of herb bread; Violet's appetite always rose when she was under stress. It seemed silly to delay answering Leo's question by then, so she began telling him about her recent Christmas visit to her family in Brisbane and the feelings which had besieged her at the time.

'I got sick and tired of being asked who I was

dating and having to say no one,' she admitted. 'But things dropped to a new low when Gavin—that's my kid brother—asked me if I was gay.'

'I see,' Leo said.

'I doubt it. I can't see anyone ever presuming *you* were gay. But, to get on with my story, by the time I left to fly home I knew I wanted to make changes to my life, but I just didn't know how. You've no idea how easy it is to get into the habit of being insular and introverted. *Very* easy not to bother about your wardrobe or your appearance as well. The truth is, I'd become a coward, for want of a better word. And lazy to boot.'

'That's being a bit harsh on yourself.'

'No, no, don't try to soft-soap me, Leo. I am well aware of what I'd become. But it really came home to me when I read *Captain Strongbow's Woman* again during the flight home.'

'What was that? Captain who's woman?'

'Captain Strongbow's. It's the title of my favourite historical romance from back when I was a teenager. I hadn't read it for years and I was curious to see if it still captivated me as much.'

'And did it?'

'Absolutely. I loved every word. And I still loved the hero, despite his being politically incorrect in this day and age. I mean, you could never write a modern hero who kidnaps the heroine then says he's going to have sex with her with or without her permission.'

'He *raped* her?' Leo exclaimed, obvious distaste in his voice and on his face.

'Well, no, he didn't have to in the end. Lady Gwendaline decided to co-operate. Still, even if she hadn't, I'm pretty sure it would have been more seduction than rape. The captain was very good in bed, you see.'

'But of course,' Leo said with an amused smile.

'Oh, I know what you're thinking,' Violet said. 'And, yes, I agree that it's just a fantasy. But it wasn't the romance part which interested me so much when I read the book again but Lady Gwendaline's character. I finally saw how brave she was. Every time she was faced with a difficult situation, she didn't faint or run away or hide. She met each crisis head-on. She wasn't passive, she was proactive. I was sitting there in the plane thinking how terribly weak I was for the way I was leading my life when I was suddenly faced with a life-threatening crisis of my own.'

She stopped for a few seconds to take another fortifying swallow of wine.

'Go on,' Leo urged. 'Don't leave me dangling. What happened?'

'The plane nearly crashed, that's what happened! For a few seconds there I thought I might die. Trust me when I say there's nothing like narrowly escaping death to inspire you to make some life-changing resolutions!'

'I can believe that,' Leo said sympathetically. 'So what were they, these life-changing resolutions? Sounds like more than just your accepting social invitations from now on.'

Violet's courage suddenly started to fail her. 'Oh…just girl stuff mostly. You know—new hair. New wardrobe. Oh, and a new car. Not that I have an old one,' she blathered on. 'I usually just drive Joy's. But if I'm going to be more social then I'll need a car of my own.'

Leo looked somewhat sceptical. 'That's *it*? Come, now, Violet, you haven't told me the whole truth, have you? What else have you resolved to do?'

Violet was about to deny that there was anything else when she thought of Lady Gwendaline. *She* wouldn't have shrunk away from telling the truth. Not in a million years! So Violet squared her shoulders and sat up straight. 'Very well. If you must know, my main New Year's resolution is not to go back home next Christmas still a virgin.'

Leo's head jerked back, his eyes narrowing as he stared hard at her for several seconds. When he finally broke his silence, his voice was clipped and hard.

'So if I come back to visit Henry next Christmas, I will find a very different Violet to the one sitting opposite me tonight?'

Violet wasn't sure why she blushed, but she did. And it annoyed the hell out of her. Leo's obvious disapproval annoyed her as well. Who did he think he was to pass judgement on her? He was hardly a saint in the sex and relationship department, as he himself had pointed out to her the other night.

'I certainly hope so,' she bit out, lifting her chin as she stared defiantly across the table at him.

'I hope you don't intend to give yourself to just anyone.'

Violet bristled. 'Of course not. He would have to be a very nice man, and I'd have to be very attracted to him.'

The waiter arrived just then to take their orders for dessert. Violet was totally taken aback when Leo announced brusquely that they would not be having dessert or coffee and could he just bring the bill.

'We don't have enough time for any of that,' he told her when the waiter hurried off to do Leo's bidding.

Violet glanced at her wristwatch which showed only seven-fifteen.

Though confused, she said nothing. Maybe he was one of those people who had to be early for everything. Besides, it wasn't as though she was desperate for dessert. All that wine had supplied her with enough extra calories for one evening. Her head was spinning a little, a sure sign that she'd downed most of the bottle. She wasn't drunk but she was not quite herself, as evidenced by the rather reckless feelings coursing through her veins.

Leo paid the bill in cash, the pleased look on the waiter's face revealing that he'd been left a huge tip. Leo shepherded her out of the restaurant and towards the walkway with a speed which suggested they were running seriously late rather than forty minutes early.

'The show doesn't start till eight,' she reminded him.

'We're not going to the show,' he replied, his grip tightening on her elbow.

Violet ground to a slightly unsteady halt. Maybe she *was* drunk after all.

'Where are we going, then?'

For the first time that night, his eyes glittered down at her the way they had on New Year's Eve. 'If you're as intelligent as Henry says you are, you already know the answer to that.'

Violet blinked up at him. 'Not really.'

'Wicked,' he muttered. 'But no matter. It's too late. I can't fight it any longer.'

'Will you please stop talking in riddles?'

'Do you think I'm a very nice man, Violet?'

'Yes. Of course.'

'And are you very attracted to me?'

'Yes,' she choked out, finally seeing what he was getting at. Good God!

'Now you know where we're going,' he said thickly, his hand dropping her arm to lift to her face. His palm was hot against her cheek, his gaze just as hot. 'Not to a show at the casino, but to one of their hotel rooms. A big room with a big bed and you naked between the sheets.'

Violet could no longer speak. Her mind was already in that room, in that bed, naked. A shiver rippled down her spine whilst her head tipped totally off its axis.

'If I were a ruthless pirate I would not even ask your permission,' he went on, his other hand lifting to take her entire face captive. 'But I am not a pirate, or ruthless. I am, unfortunately, a nice man with a conscience. Though, damn it all, it's been sorely tried since I met you. So, what's it to be, Violet? Am I to be your first lover or not?'

What a silly question, she thought dazedly. As if she was going to knock him back. But it was still a nerve-wracking moment in her life. Her hesitation to answer was bound up with her own feelings of inadequacy, not her lack of desire for him. Lord, she wanted him like crazy. But she didn't want to disappoint him, and she probably would. As much as he might want her back for whatever reason, she was what she was—a virgin.

'I promise I won't hurt you,' he said in an impassioned voice. 'I'll be gentle. And I'll give you pleasure. I'm good in bed. Maybe almost as good as your Captain Strongbow.'

But I'm nothing like Lady Gwendaline! she almost cried out. She could see that now. She wasn't as brave or as bold. Or nearly as beautiful. The thought that Leo had been married to one of the most beautiful women in the world hardly helped her confidence. She could not hope to compare.

Her body might be the best it had ever been but it was still far from perfect. Her breasts were too big; the same with her bum. And she was sure there were the remnants of cellulite still clinging to her thighs. The prospect of stripping naked in front of Leo had her stomach contracting and her heart doing somersaults.

Violet knew if she said no to him he would respect her wishes. But if she said no…

Her face twisted as she tried to picture how she would feel tomorrow if she did just that. She would hate herself. She *had* to seize this incredible opportunity with both hands. *Had* to!

Pushing aside all her qualms and doubts, Violet reached up on tip toe and pressed her lips to his. He stiffened for a moment, after which he took a firm hold of her shoulders and held her away from him, his face raw with emotion, his eyes dark and dangerous-looking.

'I'll take that to be a yes,' he ground out. 'Now, not another word. And definitely no more kisses. Not till we're safely alone in that hotel room. I need to find some control if I'm to deliver all my promises of gentleness and pleasure. I don't think you appreciate your power, lovely Violet.'

'My power?' she echoed blankly.

His smile was wry. 'One day, you'll know exactly what I'm talking about. And, when you do, God help the man you're with.'

His comment was both telling and hurtful. For it meant that this was all there would ever be between them—this one night. Tomorrow, Leo would jet off back to England and that would be that.

For a split second, Violet baulked at this horrible thought, because of course she wanted more of him than one short night. Even before the event, she knew that. It came from deep within her feminine self, that knowledge, as did another inevitability: if she let Leo make love to her tonight, she would undoubtedly fall in love with him. Did she want to risk that?

Another silly question.

Her heart lurched when he took her hand in his, but she didn't snatch it away. She steeled herself and willingly let him lead her over the bridge towards the brightly lit casino and the night ahead.

CHAPTER ELEVEN

'HOTEL RECEPTION'S THIS way,' Leo explained as he led her round the block to the back of the casino.

Violet's eyes widened as they passed a whole line of very expensive cars pulling into the kerb. When a black stretch limousine drove past slowly, Leo's head didn't even turn. Clearly, he was used to this kind of lifestyle. No doubt he'd stayed at a lot of top hotels all over the world. She'd never stayed at one. Or any hotel at all!

Not that she said so. Violet wasn't about to underline her lack of experience. She did her best to look suitably sophisticated as Leo drew her inside the huge, marble-tiled foyer where he deposited her in a plush chair whilst he went up to the reception desk. There was a small queue so he didn't get served straight away; the delay contracted her stomach into even tighter knots of tension.

Several of the male patrons walking past stared at her almost lewdly as she sat there all alone, bringing home to Violet how vulnerable women were when out on their own in a city. At last Leo returned, taking her hand and steering her over to a bank of lifts.

They didn't speak; there were other people waiting for lifts also. They didn't speak during the lift ride as they were still not alone. Another couple exited the lift on the same floor as theirs, so once again there was no talk between them as Leo led her along the carpeted corridor. Finally, Leo stopped at a door, using a key card to enter.

At least I know about key cards, Violet thought. Henry's old apartment—and now his office—used that kind of security. And of course she'd seen hotel rooms in countless movies and television shows. So there were no real surprises when she entered the room.

Everything was pretty much as she expected in a hotel of this calibre. The decor was sleek and modern, the colour palate warm and rich without being over-the-top. The walls were the colour of milk chocolate, the carpet a deep, plush cream, the furniture wooden—not light, yet not dark. Possibly teak. Her mother had a teak table about that colour. The soft furnishings came in various shades of gold, the brightest being the bedspread which covered what was really a very large bed.

For a long moment, Violet just stood there, staring at the bed whilst Leo walked over and drew back the curtains from the plate-glass window which covered one entire wall.

'Great view,' he said, and she glanced over at it. Indeed, it was pretty spectacular, especially now that night was falling and all the lights of the city had come on. You could see way beyond Darling Harbour to the bridge and beyond.

It was impossible, however, for Violet to care about the view, no matter how great it was. All she could think about was what they were going to be doing shortly, right there, in that decadent-looking bed.

Suddenly, she wanted Leo to close those curtains again. After all, there were tall buildings across the way, all with windows and some with balconies. What if there was someone there with a telescope, or a camera with one of those new powerful lenses which could zoom in on things hundreds of metres away? Gavin had been given one such camera for Christmas so she knew first-hand what they were capable of.

'Please, Leo,' she said in a shaky voice. 'Could we possibly shut the curtains?'

He frowned, then moved over, to close not the opaque gold curtains but a set of gauzy curtains which she hadn't noticed and which was obviously used by guests who wanted privacy without totally destroying the view.

'Will this do?' he asked once he'd drawn them into place.

'I...I suppose so.'

'Try not to be nervous.'

She let out a great rush of air. 'That's easy for you to say.'

Leo smiled. He couldn't help it. Did she have any idea how nervous *he* was? How *conflicted*? He'd promised her gentleness, yet all he wanted to do was rip off that sexy black dress right now and ravage her silly for hours on end. He'd promised her pleasure. But it was the prospect of his *own* pleasure which was firing his blood up at this moment. It would take a supreme effort of will to suppress his own driving needs and concentrate instead on hers.

But it would be worth it in the end, Leo believed as he crossed the room, confident that giving Violet pleasure and satisfaction would ultimately increase his. Taking her bag from where it was clutched tightly between both her hands, he threw it aside then drew her trembling body into his arms. Her eyes were wide on his, closing when his head began to dip.

He kept the kiss soft, not wanting to rush or frighten her. He didn't crush her lips as he secretly wanted to. He sipped at them. Licked them. Nibbled. Patience was the key to success here; Leo constantly reminded himself it was imperative that he didn't unleash the passion which had been building up in him all day, not till she was ready for it.

Which could take some time.

When her lips gasped apart on a raw, sensual moan, he almost lost it for a moment, almost plunged his tongue deep into her mouth without thought or care. His arms did tighten around her as he battled the urge to just let rip, fighting with all his might to contain the wild urge to ravage her mouth as he wanted to ravage her.

Finally, he dared to let his tongue slide forward, moaning himself when he encountered the delicious heat of her mouth. Perhaps if she'd remained passive in his arms he might have been able to sustain his promised gentleness. But she was anything but passive, her own tongue snaking around his, her arms doing the same to his body as she pressed herself hard against his already painful erection.

To keep on kissing her would be courting disaster, Leo quickly realised. He had to radically change his seduction technique, at the same time giving himself a much-needed breather.

Violet could have cried when Leo suddenly stopped kissing her.

'Sorry, sweetness,' he said, something like regret in his beautiful blue eyes. 'But we need to slow things down here or you might not enjoy your first sexual experience as much as you deserve to.'

Relief swamped Violet that she hadn't done anything wrong.

'Now, first things first,' he went on, having disentangled himself from her embrace. 'Do you need to freshen up? The bathroom is just that way.'

Now that she thought about it, she did need to use the bathroom. Quite badly. How come she hadn't felt that a moment ago when he was kissing her? Violet swallowed, then nodded.

'I'll make us some coffee.'

Violet scuttled off to the *en suite* bathroom,

shocked when she discovered how wet her new black lace panties were. Best she leave them off. But how could she possibly go back to Leo without her panties on? Would it be better to take everything off, the way Lady Gwendaline had after Captain Strongbow had made it clear he was going to take her that night? Violet had been startled but thrilled when her heroine had done that.

Dared *she* do the same?

Violet doubted it. To walk out of here stark naked was not within the realms of her capabilities or courage. Maybe if she had something to cover herself with…

Her gaze lifted to the shelf where two white towelling bathrobes sat, neatly folded.

Leo was just about to go and knock on the bathroom door to find out what was keeping her when it opened and Violet emerged, wrapped in a white towelling bathrobe. Now he knew what had taken her so long: she'd been undressing. Her bravery touched him, as did the fear which still lurked in her wonderfully expressive eyes. Leo could not remember the last time he'd been with a woman who was worried about showing him her body. Shyness was old hat these days. And old-fashioned. As were twenty-five-year-old virgins.

Leo could be forgiven for feeling enchanted. He would not forgive himself, however, if he ever hurt this lovely young girl. Which meant it was vital for him to protect her from her own possibly foolish self. He hadn't forgotten how easy it was to mistake lust for love when you were young. Okay, so Violet wasn't all that young in years, as she'd pointed out. But she was still a novice in her head when it came to sexual relationships. He had to make sure she didn't start imagining she was in love with him afterwards. And she might, if he let her delude herself in that fashion.

'Good thinking,' he said, quickly deciding to keep the tone of things pragmatic rather than romantic. 'Didn't know how you took your coffee but everything's there you could possibly want,' he said, nodding towards the mini-bar before striding into the bathroom and shutting the door behind him.

Violet just stood there, stunned. She'd imagined an entirely different scenario when she'd finally plucked up the courage to come out here and face Leo. Not in her wildest dreams had she imagined him leaving her alone like this. Her disappointment was acute, so was her frustration. She'd wanted him to pull her into his arms again and kiss her, not gently, but wildly, passionately. She didn't want time to think. She wanted him to throw her onto that bed and just do it!

Sighing, she walked over and made herself a mug of coffee, black, with no sugar.

He hadn't made himself any, she noted as she took a small sip and, carrying her mug, she walked over to stand in the middle of the plate-glass window, staring through the semi-transparent curtains at the buildings opposite and wondering if people could see her.

Perhaps. Probably. This last thought had her putting down the coffee on a nearby desk and hurrying around the room, turning on the bedside lamps and turning off the much brighter overhead lights. That done, she picked up her coffee again and returned to the window, confident now that nothing could be seen of her except perhaps a hazy outline. She could be walking around stark naked and no one in the building opposite would know.

Violet was standing there, sipping her coffee and thinking that she would never have the courage to walk around stark naked when she heard the bathroom door open.

She stiffened, afraid suddenly that Leo wouldn't be so shy.

Gripping the coffee mug within suddenly tense fingers, she turned, relieved to find that he wasn't naked, but dressed in the other bathrobe.

'I would have made you some coffee,' she said, surprised at how normal she sounded, 'but I didn't know how you took it, either.'

'I don't really want any coffee right now.'

He stared at her across the room, the look in his eyes thrilling Violet. She'd never experienced what it was to be wanted by a man before. Certainly not like this, and not by a man like Leo. She still found it hard to believe that she had captured his interest the way she had. Was it because she was a virgin? Did it turn him on, the thought of being her first?

'I don't really want coffee either,' she admitted, her voice low and shaky.

He sighed a deep sigh before moving to stand at the side of the bed where he withdrew a small foil packet from the pocket of the bathrobe and placed it under the lamp on the bedside table.

'I'm sorry, Violet,' he said, glancing back up at her. 'I was so intent on getting you up here that I forgot I only carry one condom in my wallet.'

Violet stared at the small foil packet, then up at him, several thoughts revolving in her head. *She* hadn't thought about protection at all! Which was seriously stupid of her. Okay, so she was on the pill; had been ever since she'd discovered it was a miracle cure for her acne. The pill, however, only protected a girl against pregnancy. Despite Leo being a gentleman, he lived and moved in a very fast world, where people slept around and were generally risk-takers. On top of that he was drop-dead gorgeous, so women would be throwing themselves at him all the time. She was sure that as a rule he practised safe sex, but who knew?

'Well, we only need one, don't we?' she said at last.

Leo almost laughed. Once wasn't going to be nearly enough to assuage what he was feeling for Violet. Common sense dictated that he get dressed again, go downstairs and find one of the gents' rooms in the casino which was sure to have condom dispensers on the wall. But that would take far too long. His need was too urgent, too powerful to entertain such a delay. As it was, it would take some considerable time for her to be ready for him.

Leo wondered how long it would be before he

could don that condom. Half an hour at least. Lord, how was he going to bear it?

You'll just have to, came the voice of brutal logic. *Because there will be no second time to-night if her first time hurts too much. If you want to have her again—which you undeniably do—then patience is the only way.*

But, best she not know that right now.

'True,' he said, and smiled what he hoped was a reassuring smile. 'Now, why don't you put that coffee down, Violet, and come over here?'

CHAPTER TWELVE

THERE WAS NO QUESTION of not doing his bidding, but that didn't stop the butterflies which by then were doing gymnastics in Violet's stomach. Her hand shook uncontrollably as she clunked the mug down onto the desk surface, her legs going to jelly as she crossed the room to where Leo was standing by the bed. By then her heart was going fifty to the dozen, her head spinning with a thousand panicky thoughts.

'There's no need to be nervous,' he said gently, and cradled her flushed face in his hands.

'But I…I don't know what to do. I mean, I…I…'

'Shh, sweetheart. You don't have to *do* anything. Let me do the doing.'

He kissed her then. Kissed her and stripped her at the same time, the robe pooling at her feet before she could object or worry about what he would think of her body. Not that she was capable of rational thought at that moment, his hot, hungry kisses quickly igniting a furnace of desire within her which made her body burn with need.

She moaned in protest when his mouth suddenly lifted from hers, not wanting him to stop, yet at the same time wanting more.

'Patience,' he muttered. Violet was not sure who he was referring to.

She watched, dry-mouthed, as he whirled away from her and yanked back the bed clothes, throwing them onto the floor beyond the base of the bed before turning to face her again. His eyes glittered as they raked over her nakedness.

'Why couldn't you have been less than perfect?' he growled.

She wasn't given any time to wallow in his flattering words before he scooped her up and placed her down in the middle of the bed. Violet gasped as the coolness of the sheets came into contact with her white-hot skin. He didn't join her on the bed straight away but stood next to it, staring down at her for what felt like for ever. And, whilst his hungry gaze thrilled and aroused her, it was not what she wanted at that moment. She wanted him on the bed beside her. No, no—*inside* her.

The intensity of her need battled with her natural shyness, making her want to do things she would never have imagined herself capable of. The urge to open her legs was powerful, only the shame of such a wanton act stopping her. But her legs still moved restlessly up and down, one at a time, each knee bending slightly then straightening, her heels digging into the mattress.

'Leo, *please*,' she choked out at last.

Her desperate plea brought his blazing blue eyes back to hers.

He shook his head then laughed, though it wasn't a laugh of amusement. 'For pity's sake, woman, don't make my job here harder than it already is.'

Violet was torn between pleasure at being called a woman and offence at the word '*job*'.

Any reaction—positive or negative—was swiftly obliterated, however, by Leo stripping off his bathrobe and giving her a full-frontal view of his startlingly beautiful and startlingly erect male body.

Oh my, she thought as her eyes took all of him in with a single mouth-drying glance.

Violet had never seen an aroused naked male before but she'd imagined what one looked like. The reality didn't disappoint, Leo fulfilled every one of Violet's sexual fantasies.

'See what you've done to me?' he said as he

reached for the nearby condom then ripped the packaging apart. 'I'd best put this on before we start. I suspect that once I join you on that bed things could quickly get out of control. I swear to you, Violet, I've never met a girl who does to me what you do to me.'

She would have asked him what it was that she did to him if she hadn't been so caught up in watching him don the condom. He didn't turn away to do it, obviously not bothered by her eyes on him. Clearly, he'd done this many times before, a thought which sparked a jab of jealousy till she firmly brushed such thinking aside as typically virginal thinking, and quite silly, under the circumstances.

She *liked* it that Leo was a man of the world. It was one of the things she found fascinating about him. So he'd been with lots of women before—so what? According to him, none of them did for him what *she* did. What a deliciously flattering thought!

Once the condom was firmly in place, Violet wondered what it felt like. Was it better without one on, or didn't it matter? More questions which she didn't dare ask. Not right then, anyway.

He finally stretched out beside her on the bed,

just far enough away so that his erection didn't touch her. She stiffened when he pushed her over onto her back, sucking in sharply when his left hand came to rest on her by then tightly held belly.

'Try to relax,' he advised softly.

Violet let the trapped air out of her lungs in a rush once his hand moved up her breasts, a low moan punching from her throat. Oh, Lord. So this was what it felt like to have one's breasts played with. It was even better than she'd imagined.

'Oh!' she cried out when he squeezed one of her nipples.

Possibly he thought she was making a protest, for his hand immediately abandoned her burning nipple to travel slowly down her body, trailing erotic circles around her navel before eventually moving lower. Violet tried to relax but could not, holding her breath as his fingers slid slowly into the dark curls which covered her pubic bone.

'Move your legs apart, Violet,' he ordered thickly.

She squeezed her eyes tightly shut as she did so, fear gripping her once more, the fear of disappointing him. Her teeth clenched down hard in her jaw, all her muscles tightening.

'Breathe, Violet,' he commanded a little gruffly.

She didn't breathe so much as pant. His fingers were *there* now, touching her right on that spot which loved to be touched. She squirmed with a mad mixture of pleasure and frustration. For she knew, if he kept doing that, she would come. Despite being a virgin, Violet was no stranger to orgasms. She'd been giving herself them for a good while now.

'You have to stop doing that,' she cried out, her eyes flinging open to find him looming over her, his eyes narrowed, his expression somewhat tense.

'Do I?' he said, the initial surprise in his eyes changing to a knowing amusement. 'And why is that, sweet Violet?'

'You know why,' she threw at him, angry at his wanting her to admit something so private.

'You'll come,' he said for her.

She bit her bottom lip, feeling quite mortified.

'Absolutely no reason to be embarrassed, Violet,' he said in that silky-smooth voice which she loved. 'I would be shocked if someone of your age hadn't discovered self-pleasure. Frankly, it's a huge relief that you're obviously highly sexed.'

She blinked up at him. He thought she was highly sexed? Was that good? It sounded slightly… slutty.

'Trust me when I assure you that you could come now and it would not be the end of things. A woman can come many times during one night's love-making.'

Violet had read of such things, but thought they belonged in the world of romantic fiction. And romantic fantasies. Even if it *were* true, she didn't want to come that way. Not tonight.

'But I…' she began, then broke off. How difficult it was just to tell him so. Not just difficult—impossible!

'Now, what does that screwed-up face mean?' he asked gently. 'No, let me guess. You want me to stop what I was doing and move on, is that it?'

Thank God he wasn't so shy, she thought, and nodded.

He bent down and kissed her tenderly on the lips, then not quite so tenderly. Her lips flowered open and his tongue slid inside. And it was whilst he was kissing her that his hand very definitely moved on, bypassing her throbbing clitoris to delve into the deep core of her sex, first with one finger, then two, then three. She cried out with pleasure, her muscles closing tightly around his fingers, squeezing and releasing in an instinctively primal rhythm. She no longer worried about coming. All she wanted was for him to keep doing what he was doing.

But he didn't. He stopped.

She stared up at him, eyes glazed, heart pounding as he moved swiftly to position himself between her thighs before lifting her legs up and wrapping them high around his waist.

'Tell me if I hurt you,' he said in a low, gravelly voice as he ever so gently rubbed himself against the entrance to her vagina.

Violet moaned. *Hurt* her—was he *insane*? It felt delicious. *He* felt delicious.

Finally, he began to ease himself inside her, his eyes glued to hers—watching for signs of pain, she presumed. But there was no pain, only a momentary discomfort as her body stretched to accommodate him. How beautifully they fitted together, Violet thought once he was fully inside her. And how beautiful he was, this wonderful man. Her first lover. Her first love.

Because, of course, she loved him. How could she not?

Violet sighed with happiness.

'Everything all right, Violet?'

'Everything's perfect,' she murmured.

'You constantly amaze me,' he muttered. 'But no more talking. I'm done with talking for now.'

Violet was glad of that. She didn't want to talk either, not once he started moving. It felt so amazing. And so right. She wanted it to go on for ever.

But of course Mother Nature didn't plan for intercourse to go on for ever. The pleasure of mating was designed for one purpose and one purpose only: the propagation of the species. Soon, Violet's hips were rising from the bed to meet Leo's, the action making his penetration deeper and bringing her womb closer to where his seed would have soon sallied forth, if he hadn't been wearing protection.

Leo's thrusting became faster and harder, his quickening rhythm bringing a torturous edge to her pleasure. Violet groaned and moaned, her head twisting from side to side in response to the sensations gathering deep inside her. Her heart thundered in her chest, her mouth falling wide open as every muscle she owned tightened in anticipation of her imminent release.

When the first spasm struck she gasped, her back arching from the bed as spasm after spasm buffeted her body. Leo clasped her close as he came too. Violet was stunned at how incredible that felt, their coming together, so much more pleasurable and powerful than anything she'd experienced alone. Much more satisfying as well. But way more tiring.

Even before he withdrew, Violet yawned, her legs falling limply back onto the bed. She tried to stay awake, telling herself not to waste a moment of her one precious night with this man. But it didn't help when Leo cuddled her to him like two spoons, his body heat increasing the lethargy which was already stealing through every pore in her body. She vaguely recalled his saying her name as he kissed her hair, and then the curtain came down.

CHAPTER THIRTEEN

LEO WOKE FIRST, a quick glance at the digital clock beside the bed revealing it was just after nine. He hadn't slept all that long, thank God.

Very carefully he unwrapped himself from Violet's unconscious body and sat up on the side of the bed whilst he tried to get his head around things. The evening was still quite young; there were at least three hours left before he would be obliged to take Violet home. The show they were supposed to be attending had started at eight and would probably finish around eleven, after which it was reasonable that he would take his date for coffee or a drink at the casino. There would be no awkward questions asked if she arrived home between midnight and one o'clock.

A lot could be done in bed in three hours…

Leo twisted round to gaze down upon Violet's sleeping form, his sated sex kicking back to life as his eyes roved over the feminine perfection of her body. He loved her hour-glass shape, the natural lushness of her breasts and the peach-like curves of her bottom. But it wasn't just her shape which entranced him. It was the girl herself. She had such character, and such amazing passion.

Despite having been a virgin, there'd been nothing virginal in the way Violet had responded to him. She'd been with him all the way, and then some. The way she'd moved. And moaned. It turned him on, just thinking about how it had felt being inside her. Her body had been so tight and wet and hot. As for when she'd come… The contractions of her climax had sucked him dry.

Or so he'd thought at the time.

Leo winced as he looked down at himself. Difficult to think straight with a hard-on like that. Time for a cold shower, he decided, and stood up abruptly. Time to bring some common sense—not to mention conscience—into this situation!

Violet woke to find her lower half covered by a sheet and a dressed Leo sitting at the desk in the corner, sipping what she presumed was coffee.

'Sleeping beauty awakes at last,' he said. 'Can I get you some coffee?'

She sat up, clutching the sheet up over her breasts.

'What time is it?'

'Nine-thirty. If you hurry we could catch the second half of the show.'

'You want to go to the show now?' she asked, disbelief and dismay in her voice.

Leo sighed, then stood up. 'No, of course I don't *want* to go to the show. But I think it would be for the best. If we stay here, I'll do things that I'll regret. You will too.'

'No I won't,' she insisted fiercely. 'I won't regret a second of anything I do with you!'

'Trust me, Violet. Now, be a good girl and go get yourself dressed.'

Violet could not believe that he meant what he was saying. What was there for her to regret?

'You're afraid I'll fall in love with you,' she said with sudden inspiration.

The look in his eyes showed her that she was right.

'It's easy to mistake lust for love, Violet, especially when you're young.'

'I'm not *that* young,' she argued. 'I'm twenty-five!'

'You're still young when it comes to sexual experience.'

'Only because I chose to be that way. Now I

choose *not* to be. Tonight. Here. With you. As for my falling in love with you, why would that be so terrible?'

'You know why, Violet. You're not stupid. I'm a twice-married forty-year-old man who has no intention of ever getting married again. You are a twenty-five-year-old girl who no doubt sees marriage and children in her future. I do not wish to return to London tomorrow thinking that I've broken your heart.'

'My heart's a lot tougher than that, Leo. *I'm* a lot tougher than that. Please, Leo, I don't want to get dressed and go to that show. I want to stay here with you. I want you to make love to me some more.'

'See? You're already using words like "make love". I didn't *make love* to you tonight, Violet, I had sex with you. There was no love involved, I can assure you.'

Violet only just managed to stop herself from gasping with shock at his bluntness. Instead, she took a couple of slow, steadying breaths. 'I never for one moment imagined there was,' she said at last with creditable calm. 'Like you said, I'm not stupid. I know the score here, Leo. I know it was just sex. But it was still incredible, wasn't it? I'd be a fool if I didn't want more.'

Leo scowled. 'You really are making things difficult for me.'

'I don't see why. I'm not asking for love and marriage, just one night of love-making. Whoops—sorry. Wrong terminology. One night of *sex*.'

Leo clanked the coffee mug on the desk and paced up and down at the foot of the bed before stopping to glare over at her with an exasperated expression on his handsome face. 'We can't stay here the whole night, Violet. Just a couple more hours.'

'I could stay longer than that,' she pointed out with a boldness which should have shocked her but didn't. 'Joy won't have a clue what time I get home, as long as I'm there for breakfast. She takes a sleeping tablet every night.'

'Well, Henry doesn't take a sleeping tablet,' Leo ground out. 'The infernal man's an insomniac at the best of times. What am I going to tell him when I rock up at his place in the early hours of the morning? He'll have my guts for garters if he ever finds out I've deflowered his precious assistant.'

Violet shrugged. 'I'm sure you could think of

something plausible. Henry's always going on about how brilliant you are.'

He glowered at her for a split second, then laughed. 'Whatever am I going to do with you?'

'Lots of things, I hope,' she said, her boldness no longer bothering her one bit.

He shook his head at her. 'Might I remind you that I only had that one condom?'

'That's not an…er…insurmountable problem.'

His eyebrows arched. 'Really? And what are you suggesting?'

'I'm on the pill.'

His mouth fell open, his eyes rounding with shock—or was it outrage?

'What in God's name do you think you're doing, telling me that?' he roared at her. 'I thought you were an intelligent girl!'

'I *am* intelligent.' Violet defended herself, her face flushing as her chin lifted in defiance.

'Really? You think it's intelligent to tell me you're on the pill at this precise moment? A truly intelligent girl would already have realised that I am having the devil of a time resisting you as it is. Now you're giving me carte blanche to ravage you silly, when for all you know I've been having unsafe sex all over the world.'

'Have you?'

'No, of course not!'

'I didn't think so.'

'And you're just going to *believe* me?'

'You wouldn't lie to me.'

He threw his hands up in the air. 'Lord protect me from twenty-five-year-old virgins!'

'Might I remind you that I'm no longer a virgin?' she stated coolly. 'So, are you coming back to bed or not?'

The look on his face was priceless.

'You are incorrigible!'

'I'll take that as a yes.'

'Not yet, missy. Why *are* you on the pill?'

'I told you over dinner—being on the pill cured my pimples.'

'But that was years ago!'

She didn't want to tell him that the fear of her acne coming back never went away. Instead, she shrugged. 'I guess it became a habit. Why? Do you think I'm lying to you?' she threw at him, stung by the thought. 'If you do then I'll get dressed and we'll go down to the show.'

'I don't for one minute think you're lying,' he said. 'And I definitely don't want you to get dressed again.'

Violet had never felt anything as powerful as the emotion this last admission evoked. But she dared not let it show in her face. Inside, however, a dazzling sense of triumph made her head pound and her heart sing. Leo was going to stay. He was going to make love to her again. But, even as he was undoing the first button of his shirt, his fingers stilled and his eyes narrowed.

'One last thing,' he bit out.

Violet's galloping heartbeat became suspended in her chest.

'No matter what I do to you tonight—no matter what I say or what you feel—this has nothing to do with love. Please tell me right here and now that you understand that.'

Violet didn't like deceiving him. But sometimes a girl had to do what a girl had to do. Because what was the alternative—she confessed her love for him and he walked out the door? No way! He was hers, for tonight at least, and nothing and no one was going to be allowed to spoil that.

'For pity's sake, Leo, you don't have to keep spelling things out for me. I understand. Truly. We're not making love. We're just having sex. Okay?'

'No, it's not okay. *None* of this is okay. But

there's no going back now,' he growled as he went back to undressing. 'Not for either of us, it seems. Lust has us in its grip—which is another thing you should learn by tonight's experiences, Violet. Lust is just as powerful as love. Sometimes even more powerful. Because lust bypasses one's conscience and focuses on nothing but the most selfish forms of sexual pleasure.

'Remember that tomorrow when you're tempted to think of tonight through rose-coloured glasses. If you can be honest with yourself about this, I will have taught you something infinitely more valuable than how to turn on a man's body.'

Violet stared at his naked body, seeing that he didn't need turning on. He was already stunningly erect.

A shudder ran through her when he walked over and yanked the sheet from her body.

'Now, no more of that pretend shyness, Violet,' he snapped. 'And no more futile chit-chat. We have limited time together and I don't intend to waste a single moment of it.'

CHAPTER FOURTEEN

VIOLET WOKE TO the sound of knocking. It took her a second or two to realise she was alone, in her bed at Joy's place, and it was Joy knocking on her door.

'Violet, are you alive or dead in there, girl? Answer me or I'm coming in.'

'I'm alive,' she called back. 'Just not very awake.'

'Well, it's going on eleven-thirty, so I think you've slept in long enough. I've just made a pot of tea, so how about getting up and telling me all about your night?'

Violet smothered a groan as vivid memories from her night with Leo flashed into her mind. Had that really been her doing all those things, things which she had thrilled to at the time but which now seemed incredible? Whatever Leo had wanted her to do, she'd done. *Willingly.*

But her willingness to please him had little to do with love, Violet now accepted. Not even remotely. Leo had been right. It hadn't been love which had driven her to obey his every command and demand. It had been need, the need to once again climb that tantalising mountain of sexual tension, to wallow in the breathless and sometimes torturous moments as one balanced on the edge before falling off into the glorious abyss.

If truth be told, she still would have been there, in that hotel-room bed, if Leo hadn't called a halt around two in the morning. Initially Violet had argued with him, saying she didn't have to go yet. But he had taken no notice of her, ordering her to get dressed pronto if she wanted him to drive her home. Which of course she had. But it had proved an awkward drive, any conversation confined to Leo asking for directions and Violet answering him.

She hadn't been able to believe the change in him. Where was the warm and passionate lover she'd been with for the past few hours? Suddenly, he'd been cold. Cold and uncommunicative. When they'd parked outside Joy's place and he'd turned off the engine, there'd been no kiss goodnight, just a stiff, 'Good bye, Violet.' At which point Violet had totally lost it, telling him he was acting like some heartless cad, even though she knew he was nothing of the kind.

Which was when she'd guessed what his problem was.

'There's absolutely no need for you to feel guilty!' she stormed at him. 'What we did tonight was wonderful. I loved every moment of it. I refuse to let you fly off back to London believing that you've done something wicked. Because you haven't. I wanted to lose my virginity, and I wanted to lose it with you. I'll remember tonight for the rest of my life!'

'That's very sweet of you to say so, Violet. Thank you,' he added. 'Now it's time you went in. It's very late. I'll call you tomorrow before my flight takes off.'

'You promise?' She practically begged him, which in hindsight was not a wise way to act. Leo had already expressed concern over her falling in love with him.

But he just nodded and said yes, he promised.

Violet went to sleep, feeling happy with his promise. Now she wished that she hadn't sounded so desperate to hear from him. Nothing good ever came out of desperation. No doubt he would be regretting his promise this morning. Maybe he'd already decided not to call.

Part of her hoped he still would call—that rosy-eyed, romantic part that clung to the fantasy of being in love with the man. But the new eyes-wide-open Violet knew that, even if Leo did ring today, it would just be out of politeness.

So don't start reading anything into it, she lectured herself. *It's over. If and when he rings, say goodbye then get on with your life!*

'I'll just be a minute or two,' she called out to Joy.

'Fine. See you in the kitchen shortly.'

'Lord, but you look wrecked,' were Joy's first words when Violet made an appearance five minutes later. 'What time did you finally get in?'

'Not sure,' Violet said with a yawn as she sat down at the small wooden table. 'After midnight.' It was not a lie. It *had been* after midnight. *Well* after.

'So, what was *Priscilla* like?' Joy asked as she poured Violet a cup of tea. Joy was one of the old school who liked her tea from a pot. 'I read in the paper that it's a fabulous show.'

'Well, yes, yes; it was very good. The costumes were simply amazing and the dancing was great.'

'And your date? Was he great as well?'

Violet's indifferent shrug was a masterpiece of deception.

'You don't sound too impressed. I suppose you'd hardly have much in common with someone of his age. Still, it was an opportunity too good to miss. Did he at least compliment you on how you looked?'

'He said I looked very nice.'

Joy's lips pursed. '*Nice*? You looked better than *nice*. You looked absolutely gorgeous! The man has no taste. So, what about dinner? I hope he at least treated you to some expensive food.'

'Dinner was excellent. The wine too. Not that Leo drank much. He had to be careful with the alcohol, since he was driving me home.' Violet decided it was wise not to mention that Leo's hire car *had* been the red sports car they'd seen on New Year's Eve.

'So, generally speaking, you enjoyed yourself?'

'Yes, it was a very pleasant evening.' Brother, wasn't that the understatement of the year!

'So you'll keep on saying yes when you're asked out on dates?'

Violet couldn't imagine herself rushing out on dates just yet. Not till she got the memory of last night out of her head. After all, what man was going to compare with Leo, either in bed or out? He might have done her a favour, taking her virginity and introducing her to the joys of the flesh, but she suspected he might have spoiled her for other men at the same time.

Violet couldn't imagine acting that way with just any man. She might not be truly in love with Leo but she *was* crazy about him. Not that she could tell Joy any of that. Well, she *could*, she supposed, but she didn't want to.

'I'll be open to all offers from now on,' she said instead.

'You've no idea how glad I am to hear that.'

Violet detected something in Joy's voice. Some strange innuendo.

'I have something to tell you,' Joy continued before Violet could ask her what was going on. 'Lisa's asked me to go and live with her and Don.'

Lisa was Joy's only child. She'd met Don, an American, during her travels overseas when she'd been in her early twenties, had married him and stayed in America—much to Joy's dismay at the time, though Joy did visit them at least once a year. They had a teenaged son and daughter and lived in a large home in Miami. Don was a successful estate agent so they had plenty of money.

'She's been asking me for some time,' Joy confessed.

Violet frowned. 'You never said anything.'

'No. I didn't really want to go at first. And then, when I did, I didn't want to leave you.'

Violet was terribly touched. 'That was very sweet of you, Joy. But you mustn't stay because of me. I'll be fine. Truly.'

'I think you will be. *Now*,' Joy added.

Violet knew what she meant by 'now'. Now that she'd started putting her New Year's resolutions into practice. Violet had to admit that last night had given her personal confidence a big boost. She was no longer worried about her looks, or whether she could attract a man. She knew very well that she could, if she wanted to. She could also see herself sharing a place with another girl after Joy left for America, someone of her own age, someone she could become friends with.

Even so, she was going to miss Joy. Terribly. They'd become very close over the years.

'So, when are you thinking of going?' Violet asked, trying not to sound as sad as she felt.

'Not straight away. I have to sell this place first. Even if I put it up for auction, that will take quite a few weeks.'

'You won't have any trouble finding a buyer,' Violet said. Newtown was a highly sought after suburb. Close to the CBD, it was a popular residential area for young professional singles, and couples who didn't require too many bedrooms or a big backyard.

'That's what Lisa said. But I have no idea what it's worth. I haven't exactly kept my finger on the property market.'

'It *is* a bit down, from what I can gather,' Violet informed her. 'But a terrace house in Newtown will always attract lots of interest. An auction would definitely be the way to go. You'll need to clear out a lot of your clutter before the open days.'

Joy nodded. 'Yes, I was thinking that myself. Still, it'll do me good to get rid of all the rubbish I've collected over the years. I'm not taking anything with me, just my clothes.'

'Are you *serious*? You're not taking any of your ornaments?' Joy was somewhat of a collector; every shelf and available surface was filled with ceramics she'd bought at charity shops and at the markets. She had a huge collection of owls, frogs and pigs. Oh, and gravy boats. She had a passion for gravy boats. 'Not even your gravy boats?' Violet asked disbelievingly.

'I might take a couple, but they're just things, Violet. As I get older, I realise I don't need things around me to make me happy. I just need people to love and who love me.'

Violet's face must have fallen at these words, though not for the reason Joy obviously concluded.

'Which isn't to say that *we* don't love each other, dear,' Joy added quickly. 'But I can see you're about to spread your wings. I'll bet by the end of this year you'll be madly in love with some handsome hunk who just adores you to pieces.'

Now Violet was in serious danger of crying. Maybe she was truly in love with Leo after all. If she wasn't, then her heart was giving a damned good imitation of breaking!

'You don't really need me any more,' Joy went on. 'But Lisa does. She's rather lonely, she tells me. Don works all hours and you know what teenage children are like—spend all their time on their mobile phones or on the computer. The last person they want to spend time with is their mother.

'Speaking of mothers,' she raced on whilst Violet struggled to ignore the very real pain in her chest. 'Your mum rang here last night. Said she'd tried your mobile but it was turned off. She asked if you could ring her today some time.'

Violet sighed. 'Will do. Now, I think I'll get myself some breakfast. I'm starving. Then after breakfast I'm going to go clothes shopping—work clothes, this time.' She stood up and headed for the toaster.

'Good idea,' Joy agreed. 'And get yourself some sexy gym clothes while you're at it. After all, your best chance of finding a fella is at a gym, not behind your desk in Henry's office. Which reminds me, have you signed up at a new gym yet?'

'No.'

'Then hop to it, girl. Don't forget the goal you set yourself before next Christmas. That kind of thing isn't going to happen overnight, you know. Not with a girl like you. And don't look at me like that, missy. I haven't lived in the same house with you for all these years without working out what kind of girl you are. You're not the free and easy type. You're the type who has to fall in love before you jump into bed.'

Violet didn't know whether to laugh or cry.

But then it came to her that maybe Joy knew

her better than she knew herself. Which meant she *had* fallen for Leo.

For a split second the thought depressed her. But then she rallied as another more positive thought took over: better to have loved and lost than never to have loved at all!

CHAPTER FIFTEEN

LEO ARRIVED IN the first-class lounge at the airport over an hour before his flight for London was due to take off. After getting himself a glass of freshly squeezed orange juice at the complimentary buffet, he settled down in an armchair in an empty corner of the room and slowly sipped his drink whilst he mulled over his promise to call Violet today.

A promise was a promise, he supposed. And a gentleman always kept his promises.

But he didn't really want to do it. Hell, no! For once he spoke to Violet again he'd start wanting her again. A perverse state of affairs, since he should have totally sated his lust for the girl during last night's sexual marathon. He couldn't remember having so much sex in such a relatively short time, indulging in all sorts of positions and every form of foreplay he knew, making demands on Violet which he'd half-hoped would disgust her.

And what had she done? Gone along with everything he'd craved with a wonderfully wild abandon which had totally blown him away. In the end he simply hadn't been able to get enough of her. And it hadn't been just to satisfy his own clamouring flesh. His pleasure had come more from watching *her* pleasure. He'd wallowed in the way she responded to him, the way she trusted him.

It had been that naive trust of hers which had finally forced him to stop before that trust deepened into something else. Leo knew he couldn't bear it if he hurt Violet. And he would, if she fell in love with him. He'd used the cold shoulder treatment during the drive home, hoping that would put an end to her thinking well of him. But she wouldn't have it, lashing into him verbally with a fiery passion which had been as telling as it had been irresistible.

Hence his promise to call her today. A stupid promise, since there was no future for them. Even if she'd been older and more experienced, she lived on the other side of the world.

But there was no going back on his word, Leo accepted with a resigned sigh as he drew his phone out of his jacket pocket. Still, he resolved to keep the conversation short and swift. He would not, he vowed, say or do anything foolish or selfish. He would encourage her to move on with her life and to forget all about him.

Violet had just decided to give up on her shopping expedition and have a bite to eat when her phone rang. The possibility that it was Leo sent her pulse-rate galloping and her fingers fumbling for the phone.

'Damn and blast,' she muttered when she dropped the darn thing back into the bottom of her roomy handbag, panic setting in at the prospect of his hanging up prematurely. If it was Leo, that was.

Please, God, don't let it be Mum!

She didn't dare take any extra time looking at the caller ID, sweeping the phone up to her ear straight away.

'Hello,' she answered, sounding way too breathless. Very annoying, since she'd planned to play it cool if he did actually ring.

'It's Leo, Violet.'

'Oh, I'm so glad you called,' she said straight away. So much for her playing it cool!

'I promised I would,' Leo replied somewhat stiffly.

'Yes, yes, I know. But I thought… Oh, it doesn't matter what I thought now. I presume you're already at the airport?'

'Yes. But my flight doesn't take off for another hour.' Leo immediately wished he hadn't told her that. Now he had no excuse to keep this call short.

'That's great. Gives you plenty of time to talk to me, then. I'm out shopping for clothes but I'm due coffee and a sandwich. I was heading into a café when you rang. Please don't hang up. I have to stop talking to give the girl my order at the counter.'

Leo smothered a sigh as he realised he had no intention of hanging up. It seemed Violet was as irresistible on the end of a phone as she was in bed!

'I'm back,' she said thirty seconds later. 'Are you still there?'

'Of course. So, have you bought a whole new wardrobe yet?' He recalled that was one of her other New Year resolutions.

'To be honest, I haven't bought a thing. I don't think I have any fashion sense.'

'Rubbish. You looked fantastic last night.'

Violet was relieved that he couldn't see her blush of pleasure. 'Thank you, but I didn't actually choose that dress. A sales girl suggested it.'

'Then go back to that sales girl and ask her for help.'

'What a good idea.'

'My ideas usually are. And, yes, I'm egotistical as well as a heartless cad.'

Her soft laugh did things to Leo which threatened *all* his resolves where Violet was concerned.

'You're nothing of the kind,' she said.

'Henry might not agree with you after last night,' he said ruefully.

Violet's mouth dropped open in shock. 'Oh, my God, you didn't tell him the truth, did you?'

'No, but I had to come up with some reason why I didn't get in till three. He was still awake, as I predicted. So I said I sent you home in a taxi after the show, then went into the casino to one of their bars, where I was picked up by this stunningly sexy tourist who invited me back to her room for a while.'

'Heavens! Couldn't you have just said you stayed for a gamble on the tables?'

'No. Henry knows I don't gamble with my money.'

'But movie making is a gamble,' Violet pointed out. Very intelligently, Leo thought.

'True,' he agreed. 'But it's not the same kind of gambling. Casino gambling is all a matter of luck and chance, with the odds stacked in the house's favour. With movie making you can increase your chances of a win if the screenplay ticks all the right commercial boxes. That way, you reduce the risk of total failure and put the odds in your favour. Unfortunately, when I chose my last project, I let my emotions rule my head—a mistake I won't make again.'

Even as he said those words, Leo feared he was in danger of doing exactly that. Not with a movie but with Violet. She'd been a wicked temptation to him right from the start. It was going to a battle royal to resist further temptation. Thank God she *did* live on the other side of the world. That should help, as well as the fact that shortly he would be starting on a new movie project, not just as producer but as director as well.

He'd dabbled with directing on other projects, once when the director had gotten ill and another time when the director he'd hired had stormed off for two days just before the shoot was finished. But this would be the first time his name would show on the credits as director *and* producer. He'd been looking forward to the challenge for weeks.

Frankly, he'd become a little bored with just producing, the same way he'd grown bored with being a lawyer. His low boredom-threshold was one of his character flaws, Leo accepted.

'So what are the main ingredients of a hit?' Violet asked.

'Sorry. Trade secrets. I'd have to kill you if I told you that.'

'Oh, don't be silly. I won't tell anyone.'

'Why don't you have a guess?'

'All right. I will. Now, let me see… A movie's not the same as a book, being a strictly visual medium. But some of the basic elements are the same. In the main, you need a cast of characters you care about. No, scratch that thought—you don't need to care about *all* the characters, but you definitely have to care about the main protagonist, who's a male, preferably.'

'That's a rather sexist statement.'

'You said your research was applied with ruthless logic, not sentiment or political correctness. Most of the big hit movies I can think of have a male protagonist.'

'Fair enough. What else?'

'Action scenes. And I don't mean car chases; I personally hate car chases. But the story should be told through action, not talk. People see better than they listen. What dialogue there is has to be part of the story telling without a word wasted.'

Leo was impressed. 'Go on.'

'Then there has to be a credible conflict. The audience has to believe that there's something real at stake in the movie they're watching. The characters can be larger than life but still have to feel real.'

'Anything else?'

'Mmm. Well, pace is very important. When you have only two hours or so to tell a story, you'd better get straight into it, then not let up till the last moment. Drop the pace for too long and you risk losing your audience. Oh, and the ending has to satisfy, with all the threads tied up. None of those up-in-the-air dangly finishes.'

'I never have dangly finishes,' Leo said, the corner of his mouth twitching as he tried not to laugh.

'That's good, then,' Violet said, oblivious of any double meaning in her last statement. 'Just a sec. My coffee and sandwich have just arrived. Thanks,' she said, not to him. 'Please excuse me if you hear slurping and swallowing whilst we're talking. So what went wrong with your last movie?'

'To quote an extremely intelligent critic I just met, it was too talky, too little pace and definitely not enough action.'

'Heavens! What possessed you to make it in the first place? No, no, let me guess—it was a book and you loved it to pieces. It was also a very long book.'

'Mmm, yes and yes. It was over a thousand pages.'

'Long books rarely make good movies. In fact, *most* books don't make good movies. Though there are exceptions, of course. I hope your next movie isn't from a book.'

'No. It's an original screenplay. But after talking to you I do have a couple of concerns. I tell you what,' he said, ignoring the warning bell ringing at the back of his brain. 'How about I email the screenplay to you when I get home and you tell me what you think of it? That is, if you don't mind.'

Mind? Dear God, did he have any idea how much she'd love that? She'd love anything which would keep them in contact. Already she was thinking that he was sure to come back to visit Henry again one day. And when he did…

Meanwhile, it was imperative that she did act cool. One hint that she was in love with him and he'd run a mile. Violet knew the score now. As a twice-married forty-year-old, Leo wasn't interested in romantic entanglements. He did, however, like his sex. And intelligent conversations about movies. She could do both of those things.

'I'd be happy to have a look at it,' she said matter-of-factly. 'But Leo…'

'Yes?'

'Screenplays are not my field of expertise. Everything I said just now was just…you know… my personal opinion.'

'Your very brilliant opinion, Violet. I can see why Henry values your judgement. You have a creative mind and great analytical skills. So, what is your email address?'

He put it into his phone as she relayed it to him.

'I'll need to know what you think as soon as possible,' he said. 'We start shooting late next week. Now, I don't expect you to do this for me for nothing, Violet. I'll put you on the payroll as a consultant for a flat fee of, say, two thousand pounds?'

'Good grief! No, no, I don't want you to *pay* me. I'll be only too happy to do it for you for nothing.'

'Are you sure?'

'Absolutely.' No way could she have accepted money from him. It wouldn't have felt right.

'Very well. How's the coffee? I hope you're not letting it get cold.'

'No. I have a sip every now and then.'

'And the sandwich?'

'It can wait.' She wasn't going to waste a second of this conversation by eating. 'So when do you arrive back in London?'

'Touchdown at Heathrow is scheduled for six a.m.'

'That's early. Will there be anyone there to meet you?' Violet asked, wincing as she realised that might sound like she was pumping him for personal information. But it had crossed her mind—a million times—that Leo probably did have some lady friend back in London. Or possibly several lady friends. The man who'd taken her to bed last night did not live the life of a monk. But, truly, she'd rather not know. Ignorance was bliss, so they said.

'No. I'll take a cab home to Wimbledon. Which is a suburb of London, as well as a tennis tournament.'

'I can't play tennis but I love to watch it on TV.

I'd love to go and watch it for real one day,' she said rather wistfully.

'Then why don't you?' Leo replied without thinking.

'I guess I don't have the courage to travel alone.' Getting onto a plane again would take some doing as well. Though of course she would have to at some stage; Violet appreciated that.

'That's last year's Violet talking,' Leo said, exasperation in his voice. Though was he exasperated at her or himself? 'Not the New Year girl. You should travel whilst you have the chance.'

'What do you mean?'

'I mean before you settle down. Difficult to travel once you're married with children.'

'I have no intention of settling down for ages yet,' Violet protested, marriage having never entered her head. 'I've only just begun to live, Leo. Do you realise that before last night I'd never been on a date?'

'I would imagine that status quo will change in the near future, Violet, especially if you keep on looking the way you looked last night. You'll have men jumping out of the woodwork wanting to take you out.' *And take you to bed.*

It surprised Leo how much that last thought

bothered him, which was ridiculous. He should be encouraging Violet to take other lovers. How else would she ever be sure when and if she did fall in love? The only way to maturity and self-knowledge was through experience.

'I do have a lot of catching up to do,' Violet went on thoughtfully. 'Most girls my age have had a dozen boyfriends by now and I haven't even had one.'

'I don't think acquiring a boyfriend should be your first priority,' Leo advised. 'Dating is good, but exclusivity can be somewhat confining. You should go out with lots of different men whilst you're still footloose and fancy-free.'

'Oh, I do love the sound of that—footloose and fancy-free. It sounds so…exciting.'

'It *is* exciting to be free to go where you like and do what you like without having to answer to anyone else.'

'Is that what *you* do, Leo, now that you're divorced and your only child is all grown up?'

'To a degree. I do have work obligations, of course. Though I'm lucky that I enjoy my job.'

'So do I. Enjoy my job, that is.'

'Then you're lucky too. Most people in this world don't enjoy their work. Speaking of work, how soon do you think you might be able to read that screenplay?'

'If you email it to me as soon as you get home I should have it finished over the weekend.'

'That's great. So, do you want to email me your opinion or would you prefer I rang you?'

Leo knew immediately that he should have told her just to email him. But he couldn't bring himself to do it. The truth was, he *liked* talking to her, almost as much as he liked sleeping with her.

Violet's heart turned over. Never in her wildest dreams had she thought today would end up with her feeling so happy.

'I think it's better if you ring me,' she said, carefully keeping her voice businesslike. 'Sending emails back and forth can sometimes take longer than one simple call.' Not that she intended to let him get away with one call. Between now and then she'd think of reasons why he should ring her again. And again.

'Right. How about Sunday evening?' Leo suggested. 'Around nine your time? That's midmorning in London. Would you be free to talk around then?'

Violet would have been free if he'd said three in the morning.

'Yes,' she said. 'That'll be fine.'

'Till next Sunday, then. Have to go, Violet. I promised to give Henry a call before I boarded and I'm running out of time. Bye.'

'Bye,' she replied. But he'd already hung up.

Violet sat there for a long moment, still somewhat stunned by this turn of events. By the time she'd left Joy's to come shopping today, she'd resigned herself to the reality that her one-night fling with Leo was a thing of the past, with no possibility of seconds. She'd certainly never envisaged any further communication between them, other than a brief goodbye call from Leo. Even that she hadn't been bargaining on.

But he'd not only rung, he'd chatted away to her at length, encouraging her to travel, to spread her wings, like Joy had said. Okay, so Violet wasn't altogether thrilled that Leo was virtually encouraging her to sleep with other men. But she refused to worry about that. Her main goal was keeping the lines of communication open with him. Already she was planning how she was going to do that. Planning other things as well.

When was Wimbledon, exactly? She wasn't positive but she thought during the European summer. A perfect time for a holiday in London, plus the opportunity to show Leo just how widely she could spread her wings!

CHAPTER SIXTEEN

THE FIRST THING that struck Leo when he let himself into his townhouse was how damned cold it was. And how empty. Staying with Henry over Christmas had spoiled him. So had Sydney's glorious weather.

But it wasn't the memories of Henry's good company, or the warm, sun-filled days, which filled his mind as he switched on the ducted air-conditioning. All he could think about, all he'd thought about during the rather tedious flight home, was Violet.

Why, he wondered as he carried his luggage upstairs, did she fascinate him so? It wasn't just because she was young and beautiful. Since his divorce from Helene, he'd met lots of young, beautiful women. None of them had ever captured his interest the way Violet had. Of course, Violet was nothing like those girls when it came to her character. She wasn't brash, ruthlessly ambitious or tough as nails. She was sweet, soft and genuinely nice.

Leo had to admit that all those rather old-fashioned qualities appealed to his somewhat world-weary self. He could understand why he liked her so much. What bothered him was why he'd lusted after her to the degree he had. And still did.

Leo rejected the idea that it was Violet's virginity which had turned him on so. He'd been turned on by her well before he'd known she was pure as the driven snow. On top of that, he'd never been enamoured with the fantasy of taking a young girl's virginity. If anything, her being a virgin had worried the life out of him. He'd been scared, not just of hurting her emotionally but physically. Thankfully, he hadn't on either score.

Leo heaved a hugely disgruntled sigh as he dumped his luggage at the foot of his bed then headed for his study. A wicked temptation, he'd called her. She was still that. Maybe even more so now. His lust for her hadn't abated at all. Continuing contact with Violet—even verbal contact—was hardly designed to eradicate that lust, or to make temptation go away.

He shouldn't have said he would send her that screenplay. He certainly shouldn't have said he would ring her. But it was a done deal now. And in truth he did have some concerns about the darned thing. Leo knew from experience that it was easy to become blind to the minor flaws of a screenplay once you were sold on the story as a whole. He'd had a niggling feeling for a while that there was something wrong with the first act, but he just couldn't put his finger on it.

Violet probably would, though. She was sharp, that girl. On top of that she was honest. She wouldn't pay him lip service. She would tell him the truth, no matter how unpalatable. Given how determined he was not to have another major flop—or even a minor failure—he would just have to grit his teeth and bear talking to her on Sunday night. And bear the sleepless nights which would undoubtedly ensue.

Meanwhile, a visit to Mandy was definitely in order. He would give her a ring as soon as he finished doing what had to be done. Sitting down at his desk, he turned on his computer and set about writing Violet a brief email, after which he attached the screenplay then sent it off. That done, he returned to his bedroom, found some fresh clothes and headed for the shower.

Finally, after he emerged from the bathroom, he called Mandy.

'Oh, Leo,' she said distractedly. 'You're back.'

A rather different response from the one he'd received when he rang Violet yesterday. Still, he understood it wasn't easy looking after two boys when you weren't used to it.

'The twins giving you trouble, are they?' he asked intuitively.

'You have no idea.'

'Actually, I do. I was a boy once. Wait till they hit fifteen.'

'I don't even want to think about it,' Mandy snapped. 'I've come to the conclusion I'm not fond of the male sex. They're born arrogant and selfish and downright lazy. So, how was Christmas down under?'

'Wonderful,' he said, and meant it. It *had* been wonderful.

'Bonk a few Bondi blondes while you were there, did you?'

Leo found himself repelled by Mandy's rather uncouth turn of phrase. Plus, the implication that he would have indiscriminate sex with not one but several females. It showed him just what she really thought of him. Suddenly, the idea of having sex with Mandy again also repelled him.

Which meant he had to tell her that it was over between them.

'Mandy…' he said, a sharp edge creeping into his voice. He'd always hated hurting any woman, even one as cynical as Mandy.

She sighed a weary sigh. 'Please don't say you want to come over tonight, Leo. The boys are still here and I'm terribly tired.'

'No. I don't want to come over. The thing is, Mandy, I won't be coming over again. It's been great—and I still like you enormously,' he added, hoping that would soften the blow to her ego, which was considerable. 'But I've met someone else.'

'Well, goodness gracious me!' she exclaimed, unsuccessful in hiding her pique. 'You mean one of the Bondi blondes got her claws into you?'

'Violet is not from Bondi,' he pointed out quite coldly. 'And she's not blonde. No claws, either. I think all the female cats live in London.'

'My my! No need to get all snooty. I didn't mean to offend. Obviously she's a darling, since she's made such an impression on you. After all, you always said you weren't interested in any kind of serious relationship, just drinkies and sex afterwards. So, did she fly back with you, this Violet? Have you already moved her into your townhouse?'

'No. She's still in Sydney.'

'You do know, Leo, that long-distance relationships don't work, not with a man like you. Or any man, for that matter. Too many days and nights without sex.'

'I'm not that addicted to sex, Mandy,' he argued, wishing he hadn't had to imply that he was having a relationship with Violet when he wasn't. But he'd had to say something. It would have been cruel just to cut Mandy off without some sort of excuse. After all, he'd been sleeping with her on a regular basis for some time.

Leo was well aware that women often became emotionally involved with their lovers, even when they didn't mean to. That was the very reason he hadn't wanted to sleep with Violet in the first place, because she would be extra vulnerable to that kind of emotional involvement. Fortunately, that didn't seem to have happened. *Yet.*

'I hope you're not upset with me,' he said.

'Not upset. No. But I'm going to miss you, Leo. You are a wonderful lover. Much better than you know. But I have to confess to being quite shocked. You always said you'd never fall in love and get married again.'

'I didn't say I'd fallen in love,' he denied fiercely. 'Neither do I have any intention of getting married again!'

'Okay, fine; no need to shout at me. I believe you. But I hope you made that clear to your new girlfriend. How old is she, by the way?'

'I don't think Violet's age is any of your business, do you?'

Mandy's laugh was dry. 'Oh, I see. She's young. *Very* young, I suspect. And beautiful, no doubt.'

'She's not that young,' he bit out. 'But yes, she's beautiful, inside *and* out.'

'Oh dear. You've got it bad, haven't you? Perhaps you'd better fly back to Sydney and take this Violet to bed for at least a month. Get her well and truly out of your system, otherwise you might just do something seriously silly like propose.'

Now it was Leo who laughed. 'I thought you knew me better than that.'

'I thought I did, too. I won't say there's no fool like an old fool, because you're not that old. But be careful, Leo. Love makes fools of all of us. Anyway, do give me a ring if and when you come to your senses. Or you get bored with having phone sex. Meanwhile, good luck. I have a feeling you're going to need it.'

CHAPTER SEVENTEEN

VIOLET TOLD JOY the truth. Not the total truth, of course. She left out the bit where she'd gone to bed with Leo instead of to see the show at the Lyric. But she told Joy about the phone call Leo had made from the airport, his request that she have a look at a screenplay he'd acquired *and* that he would ring her about it on Sunday night.

Consequently, when Sunday night rolled around, she didn't have to hide anything from Joy—only her nerves, which were considerable. After all, this was her one and only chance to convince Leo that he should continue to ring her. The way she handled this call would mean success or failure. It was a touchy situation, given she had to tell Leo that there was a major flaw in his screenplay.

Would he be annoyed with her? Would he even *believe* her?

Violet knew how unresponsive a lot of authors were to criticism over their precious work. Some gave full-on aggravation. She hoped Leo wouldn't be like that. She hoped he would listen. Because, if he didn't listen to her opinion, if he wasn't prepared to make the change she was going to suggest, then there would be no reason for him to continue contact with her, and any chance of being with him again in the foreseeable future would be gone.

And Violet could not bear that thought. She could not wait till next Christmas. After all, he might not even *return* next Christmas. It had taken him eight years to make this last visit. She also wasn't sure she could wait till Wimbledon, which she'd discovered was in late June. That was nearly six whole months away. Twenty-six weeks. Almost two hundred days and nights.

The last two nights had been bad enough. She'd been plagued by dreams, wildly erotic, extremely kinky dreams where she'd done things with Leo that she'd only read about in books; things with fur-lined handcuffs, exotic oils and other assorted sex toys.

She'd woken each morning in a lather of longing, making her wonder again if she *was* just suffering from a severe case of lust. Surely love wouldn't want to indulge in such activities? And she did. Very much so. But only with Leo, of course, so maybe it *was* still love.

'You've got St Vitus' dance, Violet,' Joy said when she got up from the sofa for the umpteenth time.

'I hate it when people don't ring on time.' In truth, Leo was only five minutes late.

Just then her phone rang. Violet struggled to maintain her composure in the face of her stomach contracting around the host of butterflies which had been swirling in there for the last half hour. With clenched teeth she took her time walking over to where she'd left her phone, casually sweeping it up to her ear as she left the living room and headed for the privacy of her bedroom.

'Hello, Leo,' she said on the way, pleased with how cool she sounded.

'Violet,' he replied. 'Have you had time to read the screenplay?'

Violet tried not to be dismayed by his lack of social pleasantries. He could at least have asked her how she was.

'Yes,' she returned crisply. 'I've read it a couple of times.'

'And?'

'It's quite a good story.' Basically, it was about

an ordinary man, an accountant, whose less-than-ordinary twin brother—a flashy private investigator as well as a playboy—was murdered. To solve his murder, the accountant steps into his brother's shoes, aided and abetted by the pretty receptionist in his office who's always had a thing for him, despite his being married. Unhappily, of course.

'Damned by faint praise,' Leo said drily. 'What's wrong with it?'

'Not a lot. The plot's original and the main two characters are very engaging. I was really drawn into their journey and wanted things to turn out well for them. Which they did, thank goodness. An unhappy ending wouldn't have done at all.'

'You still haven't said what's wrong with it.'

'It's the sex scene which bothers me.'

'The sex scene!' No doubting Leo's surprise. 'What's wrong with it?'

'A lot. Firstly, it's very in-your-face. As it stands, it would lift your censorship rating, which I don't think would be good for the film's release, commercially speaking. Far better it was lower rated.'

'Lots of sexy films do very well at the box office,' Leo argued. 'Sex sells, Violet.'

'Look, you want my opinion, don't you?'

'Yes, yes, go on.'

'Okay. Aside from the fact that I think the sex scene is way too explicit, it is way too early in the story. Positioned where it is, it will totally destroy the delicious sexual tension which is built into the plot and which should be allowed to continue for a lot, *lot* longer.

'On top of that, at this point in the story, the hero is still living in the marital home. Okay, so his wife is cheating on him and the audience knows that. But if he sleeps with the heroine *before* he confronts his wife and leaves, he becomes less of a hero. Yes, he's tempted; of course he is. Yes, he should definitely kiss the girl. But he should not go all the way at this stage. That should be kept for the denouement. Even then, it would be best implied rather than shown.'

'For pity's sake, Violet, I thought you liked raunchy sex scenes.'

'Only in books,' she said.

When Leo gave a rather frustrated-sounding sigh, Violet felt terrible.

'I'm sorry, Leo, but you asked me for my honest opinion. There's nothing worse in a romance than to destroy the sexual tension too early. And your screenplay is a romance as well as a thriller.'

'Unfortunately, I think you could be right.'

'You *agree* with me?'

'Only with regards to *this* movie. I can see that this particular scene is somewhat gratuitous. I'll have the screenwriter change it to a passionate kiss, followed by our noble hero backing off. Though it's not the sort of thing which would happen in real life. In real life, no red-blooded, heterosexual male would back off from that situation—especially when the girl in question is beautiful and sexy and has made it obvious that she wants the man.'

'I…er…suppose not.'

'There's no *suppose* about it,' he stated firmly. 'Lust will have its wicked way, believe me. So, is that it with regard to the screenplay? You have no further criticisms to make?'

Dismay hit Violet as she realised Leo was bringing their conversation to a close. She raked her mind for some other small criticism to make, but really there was none.

'No,' she said, her voice sounding as flat as she suddenly felt. So much for her finding some way to convince Leo to keep on ringing her.

'Good. Time I let you go, then. Thanks a lot, Violet. I… Oh damn it, damn it, damn it!' he exclaimed suddenly and very heatedly. 'This just won't do. I've tried to resist you. I really have. But I guess, in the end, I'm not that noble. I knew I was in trouble the moment I broke things off with Mandy.'

Violet was stunned by Leo's sudden outburst. 'Er…who's Mandy?'

'Just a friend. Don't worry, she wasn't in love with me or anything like that. We had this…arrangement. Strictly sexual. Mandy's divorced. Anyway, I rang her soon after I got back. I thought if I had sex with her I'd stop wanting you. But the moment she answered the phone, I realised I couldn't do it. Because I didn't want her. I wanted *you*, Violet.'

'Oh!' Violet gasped.

'You do still want me, don't you?' he demanded with the most corrupting passion in his voice.

Want him? She wanted him so much that it was a fierce ache in her heart. There was a fierce ache in her body too, one which she'd feared would never go away.

'Yes,' she confessed shakily. 'Very much so. But Leo—'

'I already know all the buts,' he broke in. 'They've been plaguing me ever since that night. None of them matter any more. I have to be with you again, Violet, or I'm going to go stark, raving mad. I don't give a damn about the age difference, or even the distance difference. Do you have a passport?'

'No. But I can get one.'

'How quickly?'

'I don't know.'

'If Australia is anything like England, then it will take weeks. Not that it matters. I'm tied up for three whole months shooting this damned film. Nothing I can do about it now. I'm locked in.'

'I suppose I could fly over there,' Violet said, despite not being too keen to get on a plane again so soon. 'Though Lord knows what I would tell Henry. I'm not due any more holidays till the end of the year. He wouldn't mind if I took off a day or two but it takes nearly a day to fly to London.'

'Tell me about it! Look, I can bear the frustration if I know I'm going to be with you eventually. How about Easter? I'll be finished the film by then. Could you take off a couple of extra days around then? I'd really like to show you Paris. It's lovely there in the spring. Still a little cold, but if it's too cold we'll just stay in bed. What do you think?'

All the air had been punched from Violet's lungs at the thought of their not getting out of bed.

'I think,' she said carefully, 'that I would love to see Paris in the spring.'

'Great. I'll organise everything from this end. You won't have to pay for a thing. All you have to do is get a passport.'

'I'll get onto it straight away.'

'Fantastic! You've no idea how better I feel now. It was driving me crazy, the way I was feeling. I haven't felt like this since… Well, since I was horny teenager.'

Violet didn't like it that it was just male hormones driving Leo. But that didn't mean she was going to make any kind of fuss. No way would she risk spoiling the chance of being with him again. If she was honest with herself, she was as much in lust with him as she was in love. She could not wait to be in bed with him again, to feel his naked body pressing against her and into her. She longed to touch him all over, kiss him all over.

And vice versa. That was one of the things he'd done to her that night that she'd adored. She shivered at the thought of his mouth down there, and of where he would want *her* mouth. She swallowed convulsively as a wave of heat flooded her body.

Thank heavens Leo couldn't see her. Violet knew that the worst thing she could do with Leo was betray the depth of her feelings.

'I've embarrassed you,' he said ruefully when she didn't say anything.

'No, no,' she insisted. 'I'm just…surprised. I mean, I would imagine you could have just about any woman in England.'

'That's very flattering of you to say so, but I don't want any woman in England. I want you.'

'But why?' Violet asked, genuinely perplexed by his passion for her. 'Why do you want me?'

'Perhaps it's because you would actually ask a question like that.'

'That makes me sound stupid.'

'In that case, I expressed myself badly. Because you're as far removed from stupid as a girl could be. You're very intelligent, Violet. I love talking to you. At the same time you have what I would call an untainted character, which I find irresistibly charming. I love it that you are unguarded in your opinions. I also love it that you haven't slept around.'

'You mean my being a virgin turned you on?' Violet wasn't sure if she liked that thought.

'Again, I have expressed myself badly. I just meant I've grown tired of being with women who've been putting it out there for so long and with so many men that there's nothing left for them to discover. No new pleasure. No new experience.

'And, yes, before you accuse me of double standards, I'm guilty of the same. At forty years of age there isn't much that I haven't done, sexually speaking. I've become jaded with the whole scene. To be frank, in the past year sex was just something I did to relax. When I'm with you, however, it's nothing like that. It's incredible, Violet. You're incredible.'

Violet flushed at his flattering words. At the same time, she refused to let his compliments confuse her. 'So my being a virgin did turn you on,' she repeated firmly.

He laughed. 'Oh, all right. If you insist. Your being a virgin turned me on. Big-time.'

'I'm not a virgin any longer, Leo,' she pointed out to him, struggling to contain a growing anger.

'No. But I'm still your first lover.'

'And do you expect me not to date anyone else between now and Easter?'

She heard him suck in sharply, his shocked reaction soothing her distress.

'After all,' she went on before he could say another word, 'it was you who advised me not to embrace exclusivity. You said I was to try different things, which I presumed to mean different lovers.'

'I can't order you to wait for me, Violet,' he bit out. 'All I can do is ask you to.'

'If I do that, then I will want to tell other people about my relationship with you. Joy especially. She'll wonder why I'm not out there dating, like I said I would this year. Then there's my family. I promised my mother to go home at Easter. I'll need a damned good reason not to. Last but not least, there's Henry…'

'Not Henry,' Leo snapped. 'The others you can tell, but not Henry.'

'Why? Are you still ashamed of sleeping with me?'

'I was never ashamed, Violet.'

'Guilty, then.'

'You don't understand.'

'Then explain it to me.'

'I thought I had. Henry would not approve of us. It would make your situation untenable at work if you told him we'd become lovers.'

As much as it annoyed her, Violet could see Leo was right. 'Okay. I won't tell Henry. But I'm going to tell Joy at some stage, and then closer to Easter I'll tell my family that I can't come home because I've met a handsome movie producer who's taking me to Paris for a romantic getaway.'

'And will you tell them that I'm a forty-year-old divorcee?'

'Yes. Why not?'

'They won't approve.'

'I don't care if they approve or not. It's my life, Leo, and I intend to live it. No more Shrinking Violet for me.'

He groaned. 'And you asked me why I wanted you. Hell on earth, girl, it'll be a darned miracle if I last till Easter without jumping on a plane headed for Sydney. Meanwhile, in an attempt to stop myself going AWOL from location, I'm going to have to talk to you every single day. Or text you endlessly. Or both. Would you mind?'

'I'll do my best to stand it.'

'Sarcasm now. A few days ago you were such a shy little thing.'

'We all have to grow up some time.'

'Just not too quickly, my darling. Bye now. Sleep well.'

Violet stared into the dead phone, trying to get her head around Leo calling her his darling. *Was* she his darling? Or was that just a generic form of endearment that he used with women once he'd ensnared them with his charms? Did he call all his girlfriends darling? His two wives? That Mandy woman?

Possibly. Probably. She shouldn't let it worry her. But it was difficult not to feel jealous of Leo's other women. *He* didn't have to feel jealous; she hadn't *had* any other man. Not that she wanted to: silly to want beer when you could have champagne.

'Paris in the spring,' she whispered aloud.

Paris, the city of love, and of fashion. It sent a thrill through Violet just thinking about it.

'I'll have to make sure I have some decent clothes by then,' she told herself aloud. 'Elegantly fitted garments to highlight my wonderfully toned and buffed body.'

Violet jumped off the bed with a spurt of high energy. She'd get herself signed up with a new gym first thing tomorrow morning, one which had a personal trainer who'd work her flabby butt off. And she'd find a beauty salon to visit regularly, one which did everything, not just hair—facials. Waxing. The works!

'You certainly had a nice long chat,' Joy said when she rejoined her friend in the living room.

For one brief moment, Violet contemplated telling Joy everything, but quickly decided the time wasn't right. Joy had a lot on her mind just now. The last thing she needed was to worry about *her*. But she would worry, Violet suspected. And she wouldn't approve. Leo was right about that.

Maybe she'd tell her later. And maybe she wouldn't. After all, in three months' time, Joy would most likely have sold the house and moved to America.

'We had a lot to talk about with the screenplay,' Violet explained. 'He wants to ring me again about it after the writer's made some changes I suggested.' She had to have *some* excuse for the phone calls he'd promised to make.

'Shouldn't he be paying you for your advice? Those movie people work on big budgets.'

'He did offer but I said no.'

'Silly girl.'

'I said he could buy me a return ticket to London instead,' Violet invented suddenly. 'And he said yes.'

'Ooh, *smart* girl. That's probably worth more than a consultancy fee. And you won't have to pay tax.'

'I never thought of that. I'll have to get a passport, of course. I don't have one.'

'That'll take a while. When were you thinking of going?'

'Maybe during the Easter break?'

'No point in going all that way for just a few days, love. Ask Henry for some extra time off.'

'Yes, yes, I'll do that.'

'I dare say you'll be a bit nervous, going on a plane again.'

It was testament to Violet's obsession with Leo that she'd temporarily forgotten about that. No doubt she would be nervous, flying again. 'Probably,' she admitted. 'But I can't let that stop me, can I? You're the one who said a life lived in fear is no life at all.'

'True. Heavens, but you have come a long way in a short time, haven't you?'

CHAPTER EIGHTEEN

Easter Thursday morning, three months later

VIOLET'S FIRST THOUGHT when the flight attendant woke her for breakfast was surprise. She hadn't expected to sleep at all, let alone so well. She'd anticipated that nervous tension over being in a plane again would keep her awake. But she'd been wrong; she'd slept like a baby. Admittedly, flying first class was an extremely comfortable experience, a far cry from the cramped seats you had to endure in economy. Violet could just imagine what it would be like to go from Sydney to Paris squashed into one of those!

When Leo had first told her she would be flying first class, she'd protested, saying it was an unnecessary expense. But he'd brushed aside any objection with the argument that he didn't want her arriving in a state of exhaustion.

'Suffering jet-lag is bad enough, Violet,' he'd told her with the voice of experience, 'without you being dead on your feet at the same time. We only have five days together. I don't want to spend the first two days watching you sleep.'

And neither had she, so she'd ignored the momentary feeling that it wasn't right and accepted his overly generous offer. Now, at last, the long wait was over and the moment was at hand. Breakfast was done, Violet was refreshed, dressed and sitting up once more, thinking to herself that soon she would see Leo again.

But first she had to face the dreaded landing, the captain having just announced their descent into Charles De Gaulle airport. It was impossible not to tense up as the plane slowly descended, her hands gripping the armrests with whitened knuckles. But there were no last-minute dramas. Despite letting out a huge sigh of relief after their very smooth touch-down, Violet still wasn't totally relaxed, her stomach muscles remaining tight with a different type of tension.

Sexual frustration was something Violet had come to know well. There hadn't been a day during the last three months when she hadn't at some stage been overwhelmed with desire for Leo. Understandable, given she'd been in contact with him every single day either by phone, text or email.

Mostly by phone. Just the sound of his voice turned her on.

Not that he ever talked about sex. Their conversations always involved their day-to-day lives and their work. Leo would tell her all about that day's shoot and she'd tell him what had been going on in *her* life.

Which was quite a bit; Joy had sold her house, complete with all the furniture, for well over the reserve back in late January. By mid-March, Joy had jetted off to Florida, taking nothing with her but her clothes, having given all her bits and pieces, including her precious gravy boats, to charity shops. She'd given her car to a very touched Violet who'd wept buckets at her dear friend's departure from her life.

Violet had originally planned on finding some shared accommodation, till Leo had advised her not to rush moving in with a virtual stranger, but to take Henry up on his offer to let her use his other apartment till she found a place—and a flatmate—that she really liked. Which she'd done.

Leo often gave her good advice. In truth, if anyone had overheard them talking, they would have thought they were business associates or best friends, certainly not lovers.

Only Joy had twigged to the real nature of their relationship. No flies on Joy!

It had taken her intuitive old friend no longer than a fortnight to confront Violet with her suspicions that the excessive phone calls from Leo could mean only one thing: *something* was going on between them other than chit-chat about silly screenplays!

So Violet had told her—everything. She hadn't meant to, but she just couldn't bring herself to tell Joy more lies, or even half-truths. Besides, it had been reassuring to confide in someone older and wiser than herself. She'd been somewhat surprised by Joy's lack of shock, not to mention her lack of disapproval. In fact, Joy had stunned Violet with a couple of her initial comments.

'What a lucky girl you are to have had such a wonderful introduction to sex!'

'Of course you should go to Paris, though I dare say you won't see too much of the city!'

They'd both laughed over that one.

But not all of Joy's remarks had found favour with Violet. One little homily still stuck in her mind.

'Henry's son is obviously a ladies' man, my dear, so don't expect anything to come of your relationship. Try to accept it for what it is—an experience to be enjoyed. An education. Fall in love, by all means. Being in love always makes sex better for girls. Just don't pretend to yourself that he loves you back, or that it will last.'

But she *had* started pretending just that, hadn't she?

No, no, it wasn't a pretence. It was a belief. He loved her; she was sure of it. Not that he'd ever said as much. But why else would he have gone without sex for three whole months if not for feelings much deeper than lust?

Perhaps he just didn't realise how much he cared for her. But he would. One day. It was just a question of time.

Time…

Violet glanced at her watch again. Only two minutes had passed since they'd landed. Why was it that time went so slowly when you didn't want it to? The last three months had seemed like an eternity. Violet suspected that the time it would take to disembark and go through customs would drag even more…

Patience was not one of Leo's virtues. Which was why he'd chosen not to wait for Violet at the hotel, despite saying that he would. Instead, he'd ridden to the airport in the limousine he'd booked to pick Violet up, then stayed sitting in the spacious back seat whilst the chauffeur went inside the terminal to collect Violet.

He would have gone in there to collect her himself except for the possibility that some eagle-eyed member of the paparazzi might spot him. International airports—especially Charles De Gaulle—were a favourite haunt of the paparazzi. They hung around the exit gates, hopeful of getting a money-making picture of some celebrity doing something which would make copy in the tabloids.

The last thing Leo wanted was for Henry to see some picture of himself and Violet in the press. Leo wanted to enjoy the next five days with Violet without having to worry about a single thing. The movie had been a wrap last week—thank God—with post-production not starting till after Easter, leaving him a few days to do what he'd been dying to do for the last three months.

Be with Violet once more.

And not before time, Leo thought ruefully as he glanced down at the state he was in.

Damn it, where *was* the girl? The plane had

landed ages ago. Customs, he supposed. Flying anywhere these days was a pain. Still, at least he could afford for Violet to go first class. Hopefully, she'd had some sleep overnight. He hadn't had much, tossing and turning in that outrageously large four-poster bed all by himself. Yet, when the alarm on his phone had woken him at five-thirty, he'd jumped up immediately, feeling more alive than he had for ages.

For today he would see Violet again. Be with Violet again. Just the thought had sent the blood charging round his body, unfortunately a lot of it ending up in his groin.

Grimacing, he glared fixedly through the heavily tinted window at the path she would come along. He spotted the driver first, striding ahead, pulling a black case with one hand and carrying a suit bag draped over his other.

Several steps behind him came Violet, looking stunning in a white suit, which was as dazzling as it was fashionable. The skirt was slimline and finished just above the knee. The lapelled jacket was simple and buttonless, falling straight to mid-thigh and swishing sexily around her hips as she walked. Underneath the jacket was a silky white shirt which had a deep V-neckline, showing more than a hint of cleavage.

Her hair was up in an elegantly sleek French roll, which suited her, but made her look older than twenty-five. Her face was very well made up, Leo noted, her lips a bright red gloss. Unlike most of the male species, he knew a lot about female make-up. Her eyebrows definitely looked different, thinner and more arched. But her eyes were just the same. Lovely, warm and glittering at that moment with undisguised happiness.

Still no artifice in his Snow White, he saw with a sense of relief. No pretence. She might look more groomed in her appearance but she was still the same sweet Violet who had enchanted him.

Not the sort of girl that a gentleman seduced in the back of a limousine!

And he *was* a gentleman. Or hoped he was.

The driver, who by then had stowed the luggage away, hurried round to open the car door for Violet. At the same time, Leo slid to the far side of the seat, putting himself at a safe, non-seducing distance.

'Oh!' she exclaimed on sighting him, her face breaking into a wide smile. 'You came to meet me. How lovely!' She sat down, not far enough away for Leo's liking, but he could hardly complain.

'You're the one who's lovely,' he complimented her, and bent over to give her a welcoming peck on her cheek before quickly sitting back again. 'I like your hair up. It suits you. I see you also went back to that sales girl you told me about. That outfit you've got on is even better than your little black dress.'

She beamed at him. 'I'll have you know I chose this suit all by myself! Of course, I didn't wear it onto the plane. I didn't think white was a good idea for travelling, so I carried it on and put it on this morning after breakfast.'

Leo's mind was already racing ahead to when he could take it off her. But he could hardly say that, could he?

'I do that sometimes when I travel,' he said instead. 'Wear casual clothes for the flight and carry a suit with me. So, what was your flight like? Did you get any sleep?'

Keep talking, Leo. Because, if you don't, you're going to kiss her, and then you won't be able to stop.

'I did, surprisingly. I thought I wouldn't because I was so excited.'

Oh, God. The last thing he wanted to think about was her being excited.

The limousine moved off, Leo in two minds now whether to slide up the privacy screen or not. Even as he surrendered to temptation and pressed the button he tried telling himself it was just so that they could talk without being overheard by the driver. Nothing more.

Yeah, right, Leo, came the brutal voice of honesty. *And what's your excuse for dressing the way you did this morning?* He was not in a suit and tie, but in loosely fitted trousers and a soft-to-touch mohair sweater. *This is what you had in mind all along, and nothing is going to stop you, certainly not some last-minute appeal to your conscience. What you feel for Violet is way beyond your conscience. Way beyond common sense. To fight it is ridiculous, and not what* she *wants at all. She's come here to be seduced.*

So seduce her, you fool, and stop hiding behind your gentlemanly image of yourself!

A decision reached, Leo refused to battle with his qualms any longer, settling back into the leather seat to watch Violet's reaction as the screen slid into place. Her eyes blinked wide for a second and there was a definite quickening of her breathing. But no visible panic in her face. Or alarm.

He was right. This was what she wanted: excitement. Adventure. Sex!

And so did he. But, despite the intensity of his arousal, he was determined not to hurry things. It would take at least forty minutes to make it from the airport to the hotel at this time of the day, Paris suffering from similar traffic problems to London. Time enough for more than a quickie.

'Here. Let me help you with your jacket,' he said smoothly. 'It's quite warm in here and it'll take a while to get to the hotel.'

There was no suspicion in her eyes before she twisted round on the seat and let him ease the jacket off her shoulders. He tossed it across to the seat opposite before turning her back round to face him, noting that a pinkness had crept into her cheeks. Maybe she did know what he had in mind after all. If she did, she made no protest.

To undress her totally seemed beyond the pale, but he wanted that blouse off. And her bra. All her underwear, actually. His heartbeat slammed into overdrive at the thought of her sitting there with him, naked to her waist and underneath her skirt. No, not sitting with him, sitting *astride* him, with him inside her, one of her breasts in his mouth. She liked having her nipples sucked, he recalled.

One glance at her chest confirmed that her nipples were already erect, their outlines visible against the silky material of her blouse. Seeing the evidence of her arousal soothed what was left of his conscience. Wanting no further delay, he reached out to cradle her flushed cheeks with his hands and bent his mouth to hers.

He tried to take his time. Tried to be gentle at first. But her moans derailed him and soon he was kissing her and stripping off her clothes at the same time. First the blouse and then the bra.

By then kissing her wasn't nearly enough. He wrenched his mouth away and ordered her to lie back on the seat. She obeyed without question, lying there panting whilst he stripped her entirely. Every single stitch: shoes. Skirt. Stockings. Panties. His loins throbbed as he touched her naked body all over: breasts. Stomach. Legs. *Between* her legs.

A tortured groan punched from his throat. She was so wet down there, wet and wanting him.

She didn't groan. She gasped and pleaded with him, telling him of her own desperate desire.

At last, when he could not stand it any longer,

he yanked down the zip on his trousers and freed his by-then bursting erection. She sat up straight away and moved to straddle him, grabbing onto his shoulders with bruising fingertips whilst he angled his aching flesh up into hers.

He'd shown her how to ride him that night in Sydney, but back then he'd told her to take things slowly and carefully for fear of hurting her. No such worry now. He urged her on to a more powerful rhythm. Not that she needed urging. She was with him all the way, riding him with a thrilling passion which sent him hurtling over the edge in no time flat.

Leo might have been mortified if she hadn't come at the same time, the force of her climactic contractions punching raw cries from his lungs. She cried out as well, then collapsed against him, her face burying into his neck. He thought he heard her say something. His name, perhaps. He couldn't be sure. He himself was beyond speaking.

They stayed that way for some time, Leo's arms locked around her back, her hands squashed between their chests, her soft mouth pressed against his throat. He would have stayed that way for longer, if time hadn't forced him to make a move.

'You should get dressed, Violet,' he said quietly. 'We'll be at the hotel soon.'

Her head lifted, her eyes both glazed and dazed. She blinked a couple of times then glanced around her like a person who'd totally forgotten where they were.

'Oh!' she half-sobbed, her expression pained as her face went bright red.

Her obvious embarrassment cut him to the quick. For the guilt was his, not hers. He'd been the one leading the action. He'd been the one who'd done the seducing and the stripping.

Not that he felt all that guilty. What they'd just shared had been incredibly exciting and satisfying. He could not bring himself to truly regret any of it. He didn't want her to regret it either.

'No, no,' he said, cupping her burning cheeks within the palms of his hands, holding her face, and her eyes, captive. 'Don't you dare feel ashamed of what you just did. There's nothing wrong with two adults having sex, Violet. You're a sexy girl. A very sexy girl. It's one of the things I love about you. You're just making up for lost time, sweetheart. Look, if you're worried about anyone outside having seen us, then don't, because they can't. We can see out but no one can see in.'

She just kept on staring at him with still unhappy eyes. Damn, he didn't want her to be unhappy. All he'd wanted to do during this holiday was give her pleasure. And now he'd gone and spoiled things with his impatience.

He sighed. 'I still shouldn't have kissed you till we got back to the privacy of the hotel,' he grumbled with true regret in his voice. 'I knew if I did I wouldn't be able to stop. I'm sorry, Violet. Truly sorry. It's just that I've been so damned frustrated. Three months is a long time for a man to go without sex.'

Leo could not believe how relieved he was when she smiled at him.

'I could have said no, Leo. It was as much my fault as yours.'

God, but he loved how honest she was. Because it was true, in a manner of speaking. At the same time, he could see that something was still bothering her. Her smile certainly didn't match the smile she'd given him when she'd first climbed into the back of the limousine. Perhaps because it didn't reach her eyes. Violet had very expressive eyes.

'I still shouldn't have started it,' he admitted, his eyes searching hers. 'You're angry with me, aren't you?'

'Of course not,' Violet said. She was angry with herself for being foolish enough to believe that Leo might actually have fallen in love with her. Joy had been right and she was wrong: Leo was a womaniser. Why he'd gone three months without sex to wait for her was anybody's guess. Possibly because it was something he hadn't tried before, using enforced celibacy as a type of foreplay. It had certainly made her desperate for him. Had he known that? Was that why he'd made her promise not to date anyone else? It certainly hadn't been because he would have been jealous.

Joy's advice about enjoying her Parisian holiday for what it was had been spot-on as well. Clearly, all Leo was offering her was a few days of sight-seeing and sex, with the emphasis on sex. If only she could accept that. If only she could stop hoping for more…

Time to grow up, Violet. Time to get dressed as well.

She shuddered at how it would look if someone opened the door and saw her sitting astride Leo in her birthday suit. They would assume—rightly so—that she was a very wanton creature. To claim that it was love which had made her act so shamelessly would not wash. She wasn't so sure that it washed with her. Leo had once said that lust was much more powerful than love. Violet was beginning to see what he meant. If anyone had told her that she would have sex with Leo in the back of a limousine within minutes of arriving in Paris, she would not have believed them. Lord knew what else was in store for her during the next five days!

Violet tried to drum up some much-needed sense of decorum. But suddenly, her head and her body were overwhelmed by the most corrupting excitement. She knew if she didn't get off Leo's lap right then and there she might do something seriously wicked. Because she still wanted more. More and more and more.

Leo saw her face flush as she lifted herself off him and reached for her underclothes. It bothered him that she still felt ashamed of what they'd just done. Possibly it wasn't shame responsible for the pink in her cheeks, just a return to the physical shyness she'd suffered from when he'd first met her.

And, whilst Leo had been initially captivated by Violet's innocence and inexperience, he did not want her to stay that way. It certainly wasn't good for her to develop negative feelings where sex was concerned. Hopefully, during the next few days, Leo could help her see that nothing they did together was shameful or wrong. There was nothing embarrassing about showing him her very beautiful body either. If he had his way, she'd be spending a lot of time naked during their stay in Paris. And not always just in bed.

Still, he made a point of not watching her whilst she dressed, lest it make her uncomfortable. The driver's announcement through the intercom that they would shortly be arriving at the hotel coincided with Violet reaching for her last piece of clothing, her jacket.

'Here. Let me help you with that,' he offered.

'Thank you,' she said politely.

Too politely, Leo thought, like they were strangers. Or enemies. She was avoiding his eyes as well. He had to say something to break the ice, for that was what he was getting from her suddenly. A distancing chill.

'I hope you like the hotel,' he said.

His comment forced her to glance over at him.

'I'm sure I will,' she replied, a strange glitter in her eyes like stars on a cold night.

'It's not a new hotel,' Leo explained, resorting to conversation in an effort to warm Violet up again. 'It's quite an old building and has a history second to none. It was once the home of a French countess. Then in the Victorian era, it became a rather notorious bordello.'

'Heavens!' Violet exclaimed.

'As I said, it has a colourful history. Anyway, the bordello closed down after a client was murdered by the madam. A crime of passion, according to trial reports. The madam fell in love with the man—apparently he was very rich and very handsome—but her love was not returned.'

'Fancy that,' Violet said. 'Did she go to jail, this madam?'

'Not jail—the guillotine. One headline at the time said she'd lost her head over the man. Rather tasteless, but amusing.'

'Very. They don't have the death penalty here any more, do they?'

'What? No, I'm sure they don't. Why do you ask?' He could not work out her mood. It wasn't quite as frosty, but still not happy. There was definitely a dry, almost sarcastic tone to her questions.

She shrugged her shoulders. 'No particular reason. So, what happened after that? Was that when it became a hotel?'

'It did, for a while, but during the Great War it was turned into a convalescent home for soldiers. In 1920 it reverted to being a private residence once more, bought and lovingly restored by a wealthy art dealer.

'During the Second World War, the house was seized by the Germans and stripped of everything and fell into further disrepair. After that, it stayed empty for years till eventually, it was bought by a property developer who specialised in boutique hotels. The place was totally refurbished from top to toe and opened last year to very good reviews. I've never actually stayed here but the pictures on the Internet convinced me it was just the place for a romantic getaway in Paris. Ah…here we are.'

CHAPTER NINETEEN

LEO WAS RIGHT, Violet thought as she stepped out of the limousine and looked, first up at the hotel's elegant façade, then at its setting in a quiet cobbled street with a café and a bakery just across the road. Just perfect for a romantic getaway.

His using the word 'romantic' had gone some way to making her feel better. Because of course that was what she wanted her time with Leo to be—romantic. She hadn't wanted him just to *have sex* with her. She'd wanted him to make love to her. To show her that he cared.

Okay, so maybe she'd been naive in thinking he'd fallen in love with her. He'd obviously cared enough to scour all the hotels in Paris for the right place to bring her. He hadn't just booked a big, flash hotel from a five-star chain which had all the modern bells and whistles. He'd brought her to somewhere more private and intimate, a boutique hotel with a highly individual style and character.

'Oh Leo,' she said warmly as she turned to him. 'It's lovely.'

He actually looked relieved, making Violet feel guilty for giving him a hard time just now. It wasn't his fault, she conceded—if somewhat reluctantly—that she'd started hoping for more than he could give.

'I thought a girl who was once addicted to historical romances might fancy coming to a place with some history. And romance.'

She smiled. 'You think that it's having been a brothel is romantic?'

'A bordello, not a brothel,' he corrected her. 'Apparently, a bordello was considered much more salubrious than a brothel. And much more expensive. But I wasn't referring to that. Now, no more questions. Seeing is worth a thousand words. Come on,' he said, and took her hand.

Several well-worn stone steps led up to the double front doors, which were huge and made of brass and glass. Before they reached the top step, a uniformed doorman opened both doors with a flourish whilst a second uniformed man hurried down to collect Violet's luggage from the limousine.

'*Bonjour*, Monsieur Wolfe,' the stand-to-attention doorman said as they approached him. *'Mademoiselle,'* he added with a polite nod Violet's way.

'*Bonjour*, Philippe,' Leo answered, impressing Violet that he'd taken the trouble to find out the doorman's name.

Violet only just managed to stop herself from gasping when they walked into the hotel lobby. She was totally blown away by the place. Never before had she seen anything like it, even in movies. It looked like a mini Versailles, the decor rather over-the-top but, yes, very romantic as well. Gilt-framed mirrors stretched from wall to wall, reflecting everything from her startled self to an impossibly handsome but almost smug-looking Leo. Overhead, crystal chandeliers hung from the ornately decorated ceiling. Underfoot lay a deep-blue carpet, a perfect setting for the myriad gilt-embossed antiques which filled the area.

'What do you think?' Leo said by her side.

She looked up at him and smiled. 'I think this must be costing you a fortune.'

He laughed. 'You'd be right there. But what's the good of having money if you don't spend some of it? And I'll have a damn sight more money once that movie of ours hits the screen. And all due to you, Violet. With that one simple but spot-on suggestion, you turned that screenplay from a good script into a great one.'

Violet's heart turned over at his using the word 'ours'. How wonderful that sounded: ours. Not his—*ours*. Maybe she wasn't so silly with her dreams after all.

'I can't wait to see it,' she said.

'And I can't wait to show you upstairs. Come on. The lift's this way.'

The lift was amazing, like something built at the turn of the century. Just a wrought-iron cage with a wooden floor and a door that concertinaed in and out.

'Don't worry,' Leo said reassuringly as he steered her inside the lift and shut the door. 'It's only a reproduction. It's brand spanking new and works like a dream.'

There were only four buttons, she noticed; the hotel was only three storeys high. The building had, after all, once been a home. Violet wasn't surprised when Leo pressed button number three. Trust him to be on the top floor!

'The top floor,' Leo informed her during their ride up, 'encompasses only two suites with front- and back-facing balconies. Ours has a great view of Paris; you can see the Seine and the Eiffel Tower. Well…the top of the tower, anyway.'

By the time they exited the lift, Violet was dying to see all of it.

The porter was just leaving their suite when they reached the door, Leo slipping him a tip which brought a wide smile to the young man's face.

'Merci, Monsieur,' he said enthusiastically and hurried off whilst Leo waved Violet inside.

Despite knowing what to expect now, decor-wise, her breath still caught in her throat when she walked in, possibly because of the size of the room rather than the interior design. It was simply huge, with very high ceilings and windows, a massive marble fireplace and two sitting areas, as well as a very romantic-looking dining table set for two, complete with candles. The colour scheme was still blue and gold, but the blue was paler, softer, more relaxing. No wall-to-wall mirrors, either, just well-placed wall lights and several gilt-framed paintings for decoration.

'Wow!' was all she could think of to say.

'I'm glad you like it,' Leo said. 'All the mod cons are here, but hiding. There's a flat-screen TV in that wall unit over there. No actual kitchen as such, but tea-making facilities in the sideboard along with a small fridge. People who stay here are encouraged to use the very excellent room service.

'This suite is serviced by our own personal butler who will bring meals to our room and clear everything away afterwards. There's also an *à la carte* dining room on the ground floor which you didn't get to see. No doubt you will, eventually. But I've booked somewhere else for dinner tonight. Unless you'd rather eat up here?' he added with a searching look of her eyes.

'I'm happy to do whatever you want,' she said before she realised how pathetically weak that sounded. But it wasn't a lie. She *was* happy to do whatever he wanted now that she could see he did truly care about her. He didn't just want her for sex. If that was the case, he wouldn't be planning to take her out tonight. He'd be whisking her off to bed straight away and keeping her there.

'Come and see the bedroom,' he said, smiling. 'I think you'll be pleased.'

Pleased was not the first word which came to mind when Violet saw the bedroom. Her eyes were immediately drawn to the huge four-poster bed, with its gold satin spread and mountains of matching pillows. A bed made for sex, she thought, her heartbeat going haywire as her gaze fastened on the tasselled cords which hung down at each corner. It was so easy to picture herself, naked and spreadeagled, bound and helpless against the dark desires he could so easily evoke in her. Her mouth dried at the image. How…thrilling.

'So, what do you think?' he said with an amused smile in his voice. 'A bit much, isn't it? Have you seen what's up above it?'

She glanced up, her stomach somersaulting at the sight of the mirrored canopy.

'Heavens!' she exclaimed.

'They didn't show that particular part of the decor on the Internet pictures,' he said drily from where he was standing beside her. 'But not to worry. If it really bothers you, we can always make love with the lights off.'

Now her heart stopped beating altogether. Had he really just said 'make love' instead of 'have sex'? Yes, yes; she hadn't imagined it. He'd actually said those words. A burst of happiness jump-started her heart as she turned to face him.

'I wouldn't want the lights off,' she said.

'That's a relief. I've been having wicked fantasies involving that damned mirror ever since I arrived yesterday, none of which are played out in the dark.'

Violet tried to picture what those fantasies involved. Did he want to be on top, or her? Suddenly, her mind went back to that earlier image of herself bound naked to the bed, unable to look anywhere but up at her reflection whilst he did Lord knew what to her.

There was no doubt that such a sexy scenario turned her on, but would that be *making love*?

She didn't know. She didn't have enough experience to know. But, as her mind struggled with this dilemma, she recalled all the seriously sexy things that Captain Strongbow had done to his Lady Gwendaline. A lot of their love-making had not happened in a bed. He'd taken her on the floor of his cabin. And on a beach. And in a hammock strung between two coconut trees. Once he'd even performed oral sex on her whilst she was tied, half-naked, to the mast of his ship.

Despite everything, Violet had never been in any doubt that the captain loved his lady, and vice versa.

Okay, so that was how it worked in romantic fiction. The hero and heroine always fell in love and always had a happily-ever-after ending. Real life wasn't like that, was it? What if Leo *didn't* love her? What if this was all still about lust? What if, at the end of this getaway, he said it was over between them both?

Violet had to admit that not once, during the last three months, had Leo ever mentioned what would happen between them after Easter. And she hadn't dared ask…

Violet stared at the bed and wondered how she would cope if he called it quits.

Not very well, she suspected. She loved Leo with all her heart and soul.

Maybe it would be better if she confessed her love for him right now.

Though, what would that achieve? If Leo *didn't* love her back, a declaration of undying love would probably bring a swift end to their romantic getaway. Either that, or it would introduce a tension between them which wasn't sexual. Violet firmly believed Leo was not the inveterate womaniser Joy thought he was. He was a decent man. A kind man. He would not want to use her body, knowing that her heart was breaking.

So don't tell him, you fool! Don't spoil these next few days. Take what you can get of him. Take a risk. And who knows? He might fall in love with you yet!

Violet scooped in a deeply gathering breath and let it out slowly. Yes, that was what she would do.

'You're tired,' Leo said, coming up behind her and curving his hands over her shoulders. 'And hungry, no doubt.' He turned her round to face him. 'I suggest you go have a long, hot shower whilst I order us breakfast. I know you ate on the plane but that was ages ago.'

Suddenly, tears pricked at the back of Violet's eyes, bringing a spurt of panic. Lord, but she couldn't cry in front of him! That would never do!

'Off you go, then,' he said. 'Before I change my mind and take you to bed right here and now.' So saying, he spun her away from him and gave her a none-too-gentle tap on her derriere.

'Promises, promises,' she said, throwing him a saucy look over her shoulder as she headed for the bathroom.

Yes, that was the way to act, she thought as she shut the door behind her. Playfully. Boldly.

Leo wouldn't want to spend the next few days with some blushing ingénue. He wanted to be with a grown-up woman. She was no longer a virgin. No longer naive, either. She knew the score.

But she still cried in the shower, cried her heart out.

Finally, when she'd run out of tears, Violet turned off the water and reached for a towel.

No more tears, Violet, she vowed as she dried herself. *And no more worrying about the future. Concentrate on enjoying the moment. You're in Paris, girl, with a drop-dead gorgeous man who has money to burn and knows everything there is to know about sex. Don't, for pity's sake, waste a single second of your stay here on negative feelings.* What was that famous expression? Seize the day!

Violet decided that that was going to be her motto from now on.

CHAPTER TWENTY

'COMFY?' LEO ASKED in that gravelly, desire-thickened voice Violet had become so used to during the last five days.

'Comfy' was not quite how Violet felt at that moment. You didn't think about comfort when your lover had just tied you naked to a bed, even if that bed had satin sheets and the cords used to bind your wrists to the bedposts were made of silk. All you could think about was what he was going to do to you.

Violet did have some idea—Leo had tied her to the bed yesterday as well—but on her back that time so that she could watch what he did in the overhead mirror. Today, she was lying on her front with satin pillows stuffed under her hips so that her bottom was raised provocatively. Her legs weren't restrained in any way, though Leo had pushed them apart and ordered her, quite sternly, not to attempt to close them.

Violet could not believe how fast her heart was going.

'You're quite okay with this, Violet? You seem to have lost your voice all of a sudden.'

'I'm fine,' she choked out. 'Stop torturing me and get on with it.'

His laugh was so sexy. *He* was so sexy. She couldn't get enough of him. Couldn't get enough of the erotic games he liked to play, either. This was how they had spent every afternoon, Leo's suggestions having become bolder with each passing day.

'You must learn patience, my love.'

Violet gasped as she felt something soft and tickly being trailed down her spine.

'What's that?'

'The tassel on one of the other cords. You like, madam?'

Violet groaned as he ran the tassel down over her buttocks then back and forth between her legs, making her sex clench tightly and her head spin.

'I think she likes it,' he said.

He repeated the torture several times till she was panting with need.

'Please, Leo,' she begged at last.

But still he would not give her what she so desperately wanted. Instead, he tossed the tassel aside and replaced it with his fingers, alternately invading then abandoning her body with a knowingness that refused her release whilst at the same time aroused her to a level of frustration previously unknown to her. This was nothing like he'd done to her yesterday when he'd given her climax after climax, first with his fingers, then his mouth, then himself. This was something else entirely. This was sheer torture!

'Be back soon, my sweet,' he said suddenly. 'Don't go away, now.'

When a stunned Violet realised he'd actually left the room, she called out to him. But he didn't answer her. By the time he returned several minutes later she was close to weeping.

When she swore at him instead, he laughed, then climbed back onto the bed behind her. He still took his time entering her, his penetration shallow at first, then deeper and deeper. When Violet started wriggling her hips, he took a firm grip of them and lifted her bottom even higher, enabling him to go deeper still. By this time Violet was beside herself, her muscles clenching and unclenching in a desperate attempt to find satisfaction.

'Impatient wench,' Leo growled, his grip on her tightening as he started thrusting back and forth into her with considerable force, his sudden, savage power tipping them both over the edge within seconds.

Violet made a high keening sound as she splintered apart whilst Leo roared his release, his body shuddering and shaking as his seed pumped into her. Afterwards he collapsed across her back, his hands covering hers, his face nuzzling into her hair.

'You're incredible, my darling,' he said. 'Simply incredible.'

Violet was too shattered to say a single word.

It took some time for Leo's ragged breathing to calm, after which he sighed a deeply sated sigh then levered himself off her, reaching up to untie her wrists before pulling a quilt over them both. Soon, he was sound asleep next to her, his breathing now slow and steady.

This was part of their daily routine, sleeping after sex in the afternoon before rising to shower and dress for dinner every evening. Up till today, Violet had had no trouble falling into a post-coital slumber. Now, despite having just experienced the most electrifying climax of her life, she found she could not relax.

Finally, she rolled over onto her back and just lay there, staring up at her reflection in the mirror. The light through the window was rapidly fading, the bedside clock showing it was almost six o'clock. The temperature would have dropped outside no doubt, but not inside, where the air-conditioning kept the suite at a very comfortable twenty-five degrees. Hence no need for clothes, if they so desired.

Leo often desired her to be naked for him, and not always when they were in bed. He liked to look at her, he said. It had taken Violet a couple of days to be able to walk around the apartment in the nude without feeling embarrassed, but gradually she'd discovered that it turned her on to be on the end of Leo's very hot gaze.

Not that she needed to be naked to be turned on. If truth be told, ever since she'd arrived in Paris she'd been in a state of constant arousal. Nothing distracted her from her hunger for Leo's body—not the fabulous sightseeing every morning or even the magnificent five-course dinners Leo treated her to every evening. None of it meant anything to her.

She didn't really give a damn about visiting the Eiffel Tower, or the Louvre, or even Versailles. She told Leo she did, but her mind was never on the sightseeing. It was always projecting ahead to the moment when they would return to the hotel and Leo could once again make love to her. Which he did. Every afternoon. For hours on end.

Come now, Violet, the voice of cold hard reason suddenly piped up. *What he does to you every afternoon is not making love. It's just sex, sweetheart. Hard-core sex, at that. Let's not pretend.*

Violet sighed. Okay, so it probably *was* just sex in the afternoons. There *were* still times, however, when it felt like making love. Like when they came home after dinner each evening. Leo always made love to her before they went to sleep. That *always* felt like making love, rather than sex. Perhaps because it was late at night with the lights off, or at least dimmed so that she couldn't see their reflections in the mirror above. It was much easier to pretend deeper feelings in the intimacy of darkness, when Leo's love-making was less… imaginative and more straightforward.

Their daily afternoon sex-fest was always anything but straightforward, Leo having introduced her to a variety of positions and foreplays which were hardly the stuff romantic dreams were made of. And that was even before he had advanced to the tying-up business, which admittedly she enjoyed very much. She enjoyed everything he did to her; no point in denying it. But did couples in love do stuff like that?

She had no idea.

Admittedly, he hadn't done anything seriously kinky, things she'd read about in books and which had alarmed her at the time. Violet wasn't so sure she would be alarmed now. Maybe she'd enjoy Leo inserting phallic-shaped objects into her and spanking her at the same time. Her breathing quickened just thinking about it.

Maybe she was becoming a sex addict! Maybe that was why she couldn't relax, because she wanted more. But more of what? More imaginative sex, or just more of Leo?

Violet sighed as her gaze ran over him. What she would not give to be with him for ever.

But that wasn't going to happen, was it? He'd had every chance during the last five days to bring up the subject of where their relationship was going, but he hadn't. Not that he hadn't talked to her. He had; non-stop sometimes. But it was always about what they were doing and seeing that day, never about the future.

Of course, she hadn't broached the subject either. Partly because she didn't think it was her place, but mostly because she didn't want to come across as desperate. If he wanted to keep on seeing her he would eventually say so. Tonight, possibly. After all, she had to fly home in less than twenty-four hours.

Emotion welled up inside Violet when she thought of getting on that plane tomorrow afternoon and never seeing Leo again. Suddenly, any sexual frustration she was feeling was totally washed away by the most crashing wave of despair. Tears flooded her eyes, her chin then her shoulders beginning to shake as sobs threatened.

Immediately, Leo stirred beside her, mumbling something as he started returning to consciousness. Panic sent Violet leaping from the bed and racing into the *en suite* bathroom, where she locked the door then sat down on the side of the claw-footed bath, burying her face in her hands to muffle the sounds of her weeping.

A couple of minutes later, she heard the rattle of the brass door-knob being tried, followed by a rather impatient knock.

'Violet,' Leo called out sharply. 'Why is this door locked?'

Violet forced herself to calm down and stop crying. 'I…I've got a tummy ache,' she replied, her voice husky.

'Oh. Poor darling. Is there anything I can get you?'

Violet winced at his calling her 'darling'. He *always* called her that now. But it didn't mean anything. He probably called all his women darling whilst he was tying them up and shagging them silly.

'No, no, I'll be fine. It's nothing serious. I'll be out shortly.'

But she wasn't out shortly. Instead, she showered alone, not leaving the bathroom for a good half-hour, wrapped rather defensively in one of the blue towelling robes the hotel provided. She found Leo sitting naked and cross legged in the middle of the largest of the brocade sofas, sipping a glass of red wine from one of the complimentary decanters. For some reason, his nakedness bothered her, which was perverse, given she'd been desperate for more sex earlier.

'Feeling better?' he asked.

'Much,' she said.

'Want a glass of wine?'

'No. Not just now.'

'Your stomach still upset?'

'No. It's fine.'

'Do you still want to go out to eat tonight? We could always get room service.'

Violet suppressed a shudder as she thought of how that would play out. He'd probably sit there eating in the nude, maybe even suggest she do the same. Then afterwards, it would be back to that decadent bed with her even more hopelessly turned on and unable to say no to whatever he wanted. Already she wanted to say yes to his suggestion. Already she was quivering deep inside.

Just say yes, the devil's voice whispered in her ear. *It might be your last night with him. Make the most of it.*

Violet gritted her teeth before somehow finding the courage to resist temptation. 'Actually, I was hoping we might go to the restaurant downstairs tonight. It does look splendid. We haven't been there yet, and it's my last night here, after all.'

'God, don't remind me. It's all gone so damned quickly.'

'Yes, it has,' she agreed, and turned her back on him before he could see the distress in her face.

'I'm going to make myself some tea,' she said as she walked over to the elegant sideboard which housed the tea-making facilities.

'In that case, I'll go shower and shave,' Leo said in a somewhat disgruntled tone.

Violet sighed with relief when he departed the room. She did actually make herself a mug of tea, taking it out onto the balcony, which had the best view of the city. Paris certainly sparkled at night, she thought as she sat there, sipping. She could understand why people called it the city of love. It was a very romantic setting with the river running through it, crossed by the most beautiful bridges. Then there were the parks and the gardens, all wonderful places to stroll hand in hand with one's lover.

Leo had told her the other day it was his favourite city outside of London.

'You'll have to come to London one day, Violet,' he'd also said. Not a direct invitation to come and see *him*, just the city.

She stayed sitting out on the balcony, even after she'd drunk the tea, and despite the temperature dropping. Violet didn't mind the cold, always having hated the hot, humid weather back home in Brisbane. Sydney's weather was better; at least they *had* a winter. But she'd always fantasised about living in a place where it actually snowed. She'd never seen snow. Never touched it. Never played in it. Never skied down it.

'What on earth are you doing out there, Violet?' Leo said from just behind her. 'You'll freeze to death. And you've left the doors open. Come inside at once.'

Yes, master, she thought with a spurt of savage rebellion. But she still stood up and came inside, Leo shutting the French doors behind her. He was wearing the larger of the blue robes, she noted, thankful that he wasn't strutting around in his birthday suit.

Of course, he had every reason to strut. Leo had a magnificent body for a forty-year-old. Not overly muscular but fit and lean with a wonderful shape. Broad shoulders, slim hips, tight butt and a six-pack stomach which years of obsessive rowing had produced. As for the rest of him, what could she say? Obviously he was more than adequate in that department. And he knew it!

'I suppose I should start getting ready for dinner,' she said. 'I take longer than you.'

A lot longer. Violet had learnt during the last three months that good grooming took ages. Men only needed to shower and shave then throw on their clothes. Women—ones who wanted to turn heads, anyway—had so much more to attend to. Aside from hair and make-up, they had to dress correctly for the occasion. Then there was the jewellery and perfume, all designed to compliment, enhance and, yes, turn heads.

Tonight, Violet wanted to turn Leo's head. It was her last-ditch stand. Her last throw of the dice. If he didn't say the things she wanted to hear tonight then it was over for her. Violet refused to waste the rest of her life running after a man who couldn't—or wouldn't—love her back. And she would tell him so. There would be no more hiding her feelings. No more pretending.

It would be extremely difficult, but Violet aimed to confront Leo with her love for him. Then the ball would be totally in his court.

'The time for fun and games is over, Leo,' she muttered under her breath as she strode purposefully into the bedroom to select her clothes for the night ahead.

Leo frowned when Violet shut the bedroom door behind her. That was the second time in the last hour that she'd shut a door on him. The logical side of his brain said it meant nothing, but the emotional side reacted very differently. He didn't like the feeling that she was shutting him out suddenly, that she was angry with him for some reason.

He tried to work out what he'd done earlier which might have upset her, his frown deepening as he recalled what they'd got up to in bed. She hadn't seemed to mind his tying her up again. In fact, she'd revelled in every erotically charged moment. Violet was a highly sexed girl, ready and willing to try out anything he suggested. He'd loved showing her that sex did not always have to be in the missionary position.

He'd especially loved it when she'd been happy to try some mild bondage. Most women did seem to like that. Violet certainly had, if you went by the number of times she'd come yesterday. Today had been different, of course. He'd only let her come the once. But her reaction showed it had been worth it. Delayed gratification was always way more intense.

Leo concluded their activities this afternoon were unlikely to be the problem. Which meant there was something else bothering Violet.

What was it, then?

The answer, when it came to him, had been

staring him in the face. This was their last day together. Tomorrow, they would both be jetting back to their respective homes which were thousands of miles apart. Violet wasn't angry with him personally. She was angry with fate for putting them at different ends of the earth.

He wasn't happy about their holiday ending, either. Far from it. He was even crazier about Violet now than ever.

No, no, Leo, be honest for once. You're more than crazy about her. You're in love with her!

All the breath left Leo's lungs in a rush. How could he not have known till now that he was in love with the girl?

Gulping in some much-needed air, Leo tried to think about the situation with some of the cool logic he'd always prided himself on and which had been sadly lacking since he'd met Violet.

His mind went back to the first night they'd met and the way he'd felt about her *before* lust had clouded his judgement. Her fresh innocence had enchanted him. So had her honesty and her lack of guile. Yes, he'd been sexually attracted to her but, more than that, he'd really *liked* her. Liked her so much he'd tried not to get involved with her.

Why? Because he thought he was too old for

her. Too world-weary. Too cynical. He'd cared about her even then. But he'd still got involved with her, telling himself all along that it was just lust directing his actions.

Leo rolled his eyes at himself.

Truly, Leo, how delusional can you get? If you'd once looked beyond your obsessive desire for Violet, you'd have seen that you've been falling in love with her all along!

Strangely, the realisation that he loved Violet did not bring Leo total joy. For what if Violet didn't love him back? She'd never said so which, now that he let himself think about it, was odd, given her age and rather romantic nature. It was very common for a girl to fall for her first lover, if he satisfied her in bed. And he'd certainly done that. Admittedly, he'd given her dire warnings on the very first night they'd spent together not to confuse lust with love, so maybe she thought what she felt for him was just lust.

And maybe it actually was…

Leo could not believe how much that possibility hurt him. It was like a dagger had been plunged into his heart. Once again he took a deep breath and let it out slowly, struggling now to return to logic when his emotions threatened to overwhelm him. Panic. Fear. Desperation!

Lust alone would not have waited three months for him, would it? Her feelings *had* to be deeper than that. But were those feelings *true* love? Or simply the type of infatuation that a young girl often held for an older man?

This possibility didn't please him either.

But what if she does love you? What then, Leo?

Because, even if Violet believed she loved him, would that love last the test of time? She was so very young, much younger in experience than her twenty-five years.

As much as he now wanted to declare his love and propose marriage this very night—yes, yes, as crazy as it was, that was what he suddenly wanted to do—to rush her into so serious a commitment at this stage would be wicked of him. At the same time, he refused to risk losing her. She was his. He had to keep her his. Somehow!

Filled with passionate resolve, Leo strode into the bedroom. She wasn't there. His eyes flicked to the bathroom door which was shut, the sound of a hair dryer just reaching his ears through the solid door.

'Just get yourself dressed,' he muttered irritably. 'By then she might be out of that bloody bathroom.'

No such luck. Even after he'd donned his favourite grey dinner suit, Violet hadn't made an appearance. Maybe she was having trouble with her hair. Leo knew how long it took women to get ready for a night out and Violet was no exception. Not that she took as long as Helene. That woman had been obsessed with her looks.

Thinking of Helene reminded Leo of his vow never to marry again.

But that was before he'd met Violet. Before he had found true love.

What in hell was he going to do if she didn't love him back? If she never wanted to marry *him*?

Leo grimaced as his gut tightened. Lord only knew!

CHAPTER TWENTY-ONE

VIOLET TOOK ONE last look at herself in the vanity mirror. Frankly, she'd never looked better. Now that her hair was dyed black, strong colours suited her, as did black and white. Knowing Leo was sure to take her out to dinner each night in Paris, she'd brought five cocktail dresses with her in five different colours: black, red, emerald-green, royal-blue and purple.

Tonight she was wearing the purple. Made in lightweight wool, it had a crossover bodice, long straight sleeves and a slender knee-length skirt. Not an overly sexy style, till you added the wide black patent-leather belt which cinched in her figure to a very hour-glass shape. The belt, combined with matching five-inch heels, made all the difference. She'd also left her layered, shoulder-length hair down, blow-drying it carefully to frame her face, which was made up to perfection, her dark eyes standing out against her always-pale skin. One last spray of perfume and she was ready.

Swallowing, Violet steeled herself and left the bathroom.

The admiring look on Leo's face when he first saw her was satisfying, but it didn't soothe her inner tension. He'd looked that way at her every evening so far. She could not detect any love in his eyes. Desire, maybe. But desire wasn't love, was it?

He, of course, looked absolutely splendid in a pale-grey suit, a crisp white shirt and silver tie. They said 'clothes maketh the man' but in Leo's case *he* made the clothes. Formal clothes, casual clothes; he looked great in anything. And nothing.

'What can I say?' he said with a smile as he came forward to take her hand and lift it to his lips. 'You look stunning.'

Violet didn't say a word, her returning smile somewhat brittle.

He kept on holding her hand whilst his eyes searched hers. 'I've been doing some thinking whilst you were getting ready.'

'Oh?' she said, her chest and belly tightening. 'What about?'

'Us.'

Violet swallowed as she tried to get some saliva into her suddenly dry mouth. 'What about us?'

Even to her own ears, her tone sounded coldly indifferent, which was not what she intended. Fear had made her tone clipped and hard.

His brows drew together in a deep frown, his blue eyes darkening. 'You *do* want to keep on seeing me, don't you, Violet? I certainly want to go on seeing you. Look, I realise we live thousands of miles apart. I also realise you've been the one to travel to the other side of the world this time, not me. But we could meet each other halfway in future.

'I have to go to Hong Kong in July to suss out a movie project. That's only about an eight-hour flight for you. We could meet up for a long weekend. Or a week, if you can get the time off. Then there's Dubai...'

'You have business in Dubai as well?' she bit out as several emotions started welling up inside her. Dismay and disappointment followed by the fury of a woman who felt not scorned, but used.

He didn't appear to notice, of course, his attention all on making plans for his own selfish ends. 'Actually, no, I've just always wanted to go there and it's about halfway to Australia as well. We could meet up there at some stage later on in the year. Then, next Christmas, I could come back to Sydney to stay with Henry.'

'Really? And is Henry to know about our…er… relationship?'

'God, no. Not yet, anyway.'

Not yet and not ever, Violet thought bitterly. She was to be his dirty little secret. His long-distance mistress. And not his only bed partner, either. Only a fool would believe a man of Leo's considerable sexual appetite would do without sex between the odd dirty weekend with her. She'd been a fool to believe he'd waited for her this time.

This last thought had her snatching her hand away from his, startling him.

'I'm sorry, Leo,' she said, struggling to stop her voice from shaking. 'But that won't do for me at this point in my life. I want more than a part-time boyfriend who lives on the other side of the world. Not that I don't enjoy being with you. I do; very much so. Joy said I was a lucky girl to have you as my first lover and I have to agree with her. You've given me a great introduction to sex. I will be eternally grateful to you.'

'Grateful,' he repeated, his face somewhat blank, the way people looked when they've had a shock. It pleased Violet that she had shocked him. No doubt he had thought she would just fall in line with his wishes, like the naive, silly little fool she'd been when they'd first met. But she wasn't that girl any longer. No, siree. Not even remotely!

She even managed to find a coolly polite smile. 'Yes, of course I'm grateful. I'm sure lots of girls have simply dreadful experiences when they first try sex. I'm glad now that fate made me wait for a man like you. Someone older and very experienced. I've enjoyed our time together very much, Leo, but it's time for me to move on. Thank you for your kind offers but I must decline.'

He just stared at her and Violet was taken aback by the expression in his eyes. If she didn't know better, she would say he looked quite devastated. But then he smiled, a strange, rather sad smile.

'How ironic,' he murmured.

'What is?' she said sharply, never having liked it when people made cryptic statements like that without further explanation. Henry did it all the time.

He shrugged and turned away from her. 'Best you don't know, Violet.'

'I hate it when people do that to me,' she threw after him. 'It's totally selfish. But then you're a selfish man, aren't you?' she snapped, the temper she'd been trying to control finally getting the better of her. 'Selfish and arrogant and bloody presumptuous.

'You thought I'd just do everything you wanted me to do, didn't you, without offering me anything in return? Nothing of any real value, anyway. No commitment. No caring. Certainly not love. My God, do you even know what love is? I doubt it. All you feel where women are concerned is lust!'

By then Violet felt like she was going to explode, but she hadn't finished with him yet. 'You thought you could buy my body with your first-class flights and your fancy holidays and your five-star restaurants. Well, let me tell you that you can't, you cold-blooded bastard! I'm not for sale!'

Violet was aware that Leo had stood rooted to the spot during her tirade, his back to her. So, when he turned around and she saw he was half-smiling, her blood pressure went up another notch.

'You love me, don't you?' he said, his simple statement of fact smashing Violet's defences to pieces. No point in denying it now. He *knew*.

'Of course I love you, you stupid man,' she blurted out. 'Why do you think I agreed to come here in the first place? What kind of girl do you think I am?'

'I'll tell you what kind of girl I think you are. I think you are the nicest, sweetest, smartest, sexiest girl I've ever met and I love you more than I can say.'

Violet's mouth dropped open, all words failing her.

'I didn't want to say anything earlier because I didn't want to rush you,' he went on, walking up to her and taking her frozen hands in his. 'You're right about my being stupid. I didn't realise how it would sound, suggesting we meet up all over the world only once in a while.

'I'm so sorry, Violet, for making you think I only wanted you as a part-time mistress. That's not what I want at all. I want so much more. First, I don't want you to go home. I want you to come back to London to live with me. No, no, that's not what I really want, though it would do for starters. What I really want is for you to be my wife.'

'Your wife!'

'Yes. My wife. So, for pity's sake, tell me now if that's not what *you* want,' he said fiercely, his fingers crushing hers. 'Don't leave me dangling. I told you once before I'm not fond of dangling.'

'Oh, Leo,' she cried, tears flooding her eyes.

'God help me, is that a yes or a no?'

When she nodded, he swept her into his arms, not kissing her, just holding her tight, cradling her head against his shoulder. 'I never believed I could feel this way,' he told her in an emotion-roughened voice. 'When I thought you didn't love me just now, or even care about me at all, my whole world was in imminent danger of collapsing. But then you started tearing strips off me and I knew immediately that I was wrong.'

Violet drew back and smiled up into his handsome face. 'How could I not fall in love with the nicest, sweetest, smartest, sexiest man in the whole wide world?'

He laughed. 'What happened to selfish, arrogant and presumptuous?'

She shook her head from side to side. 'You're none of those things.'

'Yes, I am. Often.'

'Well, none of us are perfect, Leo. I'm certainly not.'

'You're perfect to me.'

She sighed with happiness. 'I think I should marry you quick before you find out otherwise.'

'I think you should too. But are you sure, Violet?'

'I'm absolutely sure.' Silly man. Why on earth wouldn't she be sure? It was her dream come true!

'In that case, there's something I have to do straight away. *Before* we go down to dinner.'

'What's that?'

'Ring Henry.'

Violet winced. 'Oh, dear. He's not going to be happy, is he?'

'He might surprise you.'

He did. After an initial few seconds of shock, followed by some rather sticky questions, Henry came round to acceptance of the situation with good grace and, Violet thought after she talked to him, sincere congratulations. He seemed genuinely happy for them both, which made her even happier. She would have hated for Henry to disapprove.

'I could still work for you from London,' she suggested to him. 'You don't really need an assistant on site, not with email.'

'An excellent suggestion, and one which I aim to take you up on.'

'Great,' Violet said. She didn't want to give up work and become a lady of leisure. That didn't appeal to her at all. 'You could sell that other apartment as well,' she added.

'No. I think I'll hang on to that. It's a good investment. Besides, I like working in the city. There are a lot more restaurants at hand for my client lunches.'

'Oh, you and your client lunches!'

'I'll have you know, missy, I do my best work over lunch. Now, off you go. I'm sure you have better things to do than talk to your future father-in-law. Give my love to Leo and tell him that I think this is by far the best move he's ever made in his life. I'm very proud of him.'

'Your father said to tell you that he's very proud of you,' Violet said after she hung up.

'Wow,' Leo said. 'He must really like you, my darling. So, do you want to ring your folks and tell them too?'

'No. Not tonight. That can wait. They already know I'm here in Paris with you. I didn't keep you a secret, Leo. What about your son?'

'Liam can wait too. Tonight should be all about us, Violet. I just want to wallow in our love for each other. You sure you still want to go down to dinner?'

'Yes, yes I do,' she said after a moment's temptation. 'I'm starving.'

'But I thought you had a stomach ache earlier.'

'Nah. I was sitting on the edge of the bath, crying.'

'Oh, Violet. I'm so sorry for letting you think I didn't care about you. I always did, you know, right from the start. I just didn't realise how much. But, when the penny dropped earlier this evening, I should have said I loved you straight away. I guess I was afraid to.'

Violet was touched that Leo would admit something like that. He always seemed so sure of himself. But it was a sign of her new found maturity that she understood that no one *was* perfect, even the man she'd imagined was just that.

'Then tell me now, Leo,' she said softly.

'I love you, my darling Violet.'

'And I love you, my darling Leo,' she returned, entwining her arms around his neck and bringing her mouth up to his.

They kissed. Not wildly or hungrily, but lovingly. Then they went down to dinner where they sat at length over a magnificent meal, making plans for their future together.

'What about children, Leo?' she asked him over

coffee and mints. 'I would like to have at least one child.'

'I can't think of anything I'd like better. I've always enjoyed being a father. Liam was the best thing to come out of my first marriage.'

'And your second marriage, Leo? Would you mind if I asked you about that?'

He sighed. 'It's not a pretty story.'

'I don't care. I need to know what happened or I'll be curious about it for ever.'

'Fair enough. Look, I fancied myself in love with Helene. It's amazing the tricks a male ego can play on you. But love had nothing to do with that relationship. It was all about image and status. When we met, I'd just won another award for best picture and Helene had just been voted the most beautiful actress in the world by some glossy magazine. They forgot to mention that she was also the most vain, amoral, ambitious woman I have ever met. And, trust me, I've met quite a few.'

'Heavens! That's so different to what I imagined. So what happened?'

Leo shrugged. 'Less than a year after we were married, I walked in on her screwing her latest leading man in her dressing room. She claimed it meant nothing.'

'Oh, Leo. How distressing for you!'

'Only for a few egotistical moments. Then I realised that I didn't really give a damn. Though I have to confess my lack of emotion left me wondering if I had any feelings left in me at all. That's one of the reasons I thought I'd never fall in love again. I had no idea till I met you that I'd never actually *been* in love.'

'Oh…I like the sound of that. Okay, enough talk of the past. Back to us. When do you want to get married?'

'I'd marry you tomorrow if we could. But I understand that weddings take a little longer than that to organise.'

'True. And I would want to get married back in Australia, if you don't mind, so that my family could attend.'

'Fair enough. So, about this baby business. Do you want to wait till we get married or start trying straight away?'

'I'm not sure. If I say yes to straight away, I'll have to go off the pill.'

'True. Is there a problem with that?'

'Well, yes, sort of. What if the pimples come back?'

Leo's heart turned over when he saw the immediate panic in her eyes. Poor darling. As if he would love her any less with a few pimples. But he could see that it would definitely bother her. Those teenage scars had indeed run deep.

'I very much doubt that would happen now, Violet,' he reassured her. 'But if you're worried you can go see a skin specialist first. London has the best doctors in the world.'

'The best movie directors in the world too,' she told him with a warm smile.

Leo was touched by her compliment, and by her obvious love for him. He still could not believe his luck in finding this wonderful girl to spend the rest of his life with. She was so very special. So unique.

'I *could* be the best in the world,' he said warmly, 'with you at my side. We make a great team. Now, if you've had enough of that coffee, it's high time we retired to our boudoir and celebrated our engagement in a more…private fashion.'

Violet's pulse-rate soared as they both stood up and Leo put his hand in hers.

'You're not going to tie me up again, are you?' she whispered to him as he led her away.

'Not unless you want me to,' he whispered back.

'No, not tonight. Tonight I want you to make love to me with our arms around each other and our eyes meeting.'

'You mean in the missionary position?'

'That's a silly name for it. I'm renaming it the loving position.'

By then they'd reached the lift and didn't have to whisper.

'Okay,' Leo said. 'I just hope I can remember how to do it that way. It's been a while…'

Violet glared up at him and he laughed.

They made love in the loving position not once but twice, Leo realising as he drifted off to sleep afterwards that sex was extremely satisfying that way when the couple loved each other.

Which they did.

Oh yes, they did indeed.

CHAPTER TWENTY-TWO

New Year's Eve, eight months later

'YOU MAKE A VERY beautiful bride,' Violet's mother said. 'I just love you in that dress. It's glorious. Don't you think so, Vanessa?'

'Absolutely,' Vanessa replied warmly. 'Leo's one lucky man.'

'I think I'm the lucky one here,' Violet said as she thought of the man she was about to marry. He was everything she'd ever wanted in a husband, and more. Not just strong, sexy and successful, but sensitive too. And generous to a fault. He'd paid for her whole family to fly down to Sydney for their wedding. He'd also paid too for them to stay at a five-star hotel and be chauffeured around in not one, but two limousines. There were, after all, eight of them now that Gavin had snared himself a fiancée of his own, a truly nice girl who was obviously in awe of the man her future sister-in-law was marrying tonight.

She wasn't the only one. Her parents thought Leo was the ant's pants. So did Gavin and Steve. Vanessa was the only one in her family ever to have expressed any doubts over their relationship. Initially, she'd worried that Leo might be too much a man of the world for Violet. But once she'd met Leo, and he'd worked his charm on her, all her doubts had disappeared.

A tap on the door of Henry's bedroom had the three women turning to see who it was. Henry popped his head inside.

'Not to worry,' he said smilingly. 'It's only me, not the groom. I do know the tradition, girls. But I have a little surprise for Violet. And here she is!'

So saying, he pushed the door open and in walked Joy, looking extremely elegant in pale grey.

'Oh!' Violet cried, delighted almost beyond words. 'But…but…' Joy had been invited, of course, but she'd said she couldn't come, that her arthritis was too bad to sit on a plane that long.

Joy grinned. 'At the last minute I decided to take up Leo's offer to fly first class. He's a very persuasive man, that fiancé of yours.'

Violet laughed. 'Tell me about it. But I'm so glad

to see you,' she said, coming forward to give her dear friend a big hug.

'Me too, love. So this is your mum and your sister, I presume? What a good-looking family you have.'

Violet had to smile whilst her mother and sister preened under Joy's compliment. Leo wasn't the only charmer in her life, it seemed.

Another tap on the door sent all four women whirling to face it.

'Just me again,' Henry said as the door opened once more. 'It's almost time, Violet. After all, we want to get through the ceremony before those fireworks go off at nine. Otherwise we won't hear a single word.'

'Okay. Mum, you go and tell Dad to come in. Vanessa, you help me get these flowers in my hair. And Joy, you go with Henry and make sure everyone is assembled out on the balcony.' They would easily fit, Violet knew, the only guests being her family, along with Henry, Liam and Liam's new girlfriend. She hadn't wanted to invite any would-bes if they could-bes.

'I can't believe how confident you've become,' Vanessa said after the others had departed. 'And how beautiful.'

Tears pricked at Violet's eyes at her sister's words. They were sweet words, admittedly, but they reminded Violet of a time when she hadn't been at all beautiful, let alone confident. She supposed it was rather amazing, the change in her. Amazing, but rather wonderful. Certainly nothing to cry about.

'Guess what?' she said happily. 'I changed my old pill to the mini-pill and look—not a pimple in sight!'

'You have fantastic skin now, Violet. I envy you. I'm beginning to get wrinkles.'

'Oh, rubbish. You are not. You're what they call a yummy mummy. I hope I keep my figure the way you have after I have children.'

'That's one thing I wanted to ask you, but didn't dare. Does Leo want children?'

'Absolutely. He'd have one tomorrow but I decided I wanted him to myself for a while.'

'I don't blame you. He's utterly gorgeous. I'd ask you what he's like in bed but I don't have to. It's written all over your face.'

For the first time in ages, Violet blushed.

Vanessa's eyebrows lifted. 'That good, eh?'

'Er...yes.'

'I'd envy you if Steve wasn't bloody brilliant in

the sack. The things he does! I'd tell you, except I don't want to shock my little sister.'

Violet was still smiling to herself when her father walked in.

'Well, blow me down!' her dad said straight away. 'How did an ugly old coot like me have two such beautiful daughters?'

Violet and Vanessa exchanged shocked glances. They'd never heard their father say that many words in a row before, let alone complimentary ones. Maybe some charm had rubbed off from Leo and Henry.

'So, are you ready, girls? Henry says it's time to get this show on the road.'

'We're ready,' they both chorused and picked up their bouquets. Vanessa's was a small pink-and-white posy whilst Violet carried a long trailing bouquet of white roses.

Leo stood there, desperately trying to look cool and sophisticated in his James Bond tuxedo whilst he waited for Violet to make an appearance. But everything in his body was tingling with anticipation. Eight long months he'd waited for this night, longer than he'd wanted. But he'd bowed to Violet's wishes that they marry on the same night and in the same setting that they'd met, a romantic notion which he hadn't really shared. Till now. Now it did seem right. And yes, very romantic.

In truth, there wasn't anything Leo wouldn't do to please Violet, even waiting this long to marry her, which had been a stretch for his patience.

In the back of his mind, however, he'd known it was wise to wait awhile, thereby giving Violet a chance to be sure about her feelings. It would have been very selfish of him to rush someone so young and inexperienced into marriage. So he'd waited and watched. And now he too was sure. She loved him as much as he loved her. Maybe even more. She was a dream to live with, and to work with, an asset to his life in more ways than one.

She was a dream to make love to as well, always so responsive and willing. And quite naughty at times. She'd actually bought him a pair of fur-lined handcuffs for his birthday. When he'd pretended to be shocked she'd said not to worry, that it was false fur.

He smiled at the recollection. Wicked minx!

Henry dug him in the ribs suddenly, snapping Leo back to the present. The music had started up, not traditional bridal music, but a song which

Leo had chosen: Stevie Wonder singing “Isn’t She Lovely?”

Vanessa came out onto the balcony first, her pale-pink dress suiting her blonde prettiness. She smiled at him as she passed, although by then Leo’s attention was all on the bride.

Leo sucked in a breath sharply when he first caught sight of Violet. He wasn’t sure what he’d been expecting her to wear, possibly something satiny with a beaded bodice, a big skirt and a long veil with a train. Brides seemed to like that combination.

He should have known his Violet would be different.

Yes, the dress was bridal white. But the style was very simple and very elegant, the skirt long and slender, the fitted bodice strapless without being too low-cut. She didn’t wear a veil. Instead, some lovely white flowers decorated her hair which had grown longer during the last eight and a half months, falling almost to her shoulder blades. Her jewellery was minimal, just the long, diamond-drop earrings which he’d bought for her when *Double Trouble* had opened to rave reviews.

How beautiful she looked. And how happy, her skin glowing and her eyes sparkling.

Beside her walked her father, proud as punch. He smiled at Leo as he gave his daughter's hand to him, whispering, 'Look after her,' at the same time.

Leo's fingers tightened around Violet's.

Look after her? He would *die* for her!

The elderly celebrant—a friend of Henry—stepped forward.

'We are gathered here tonight,' he said in a deep, rich voice, 'to witness the joining in marriage of Leo and Violet. They did not want to say the traditional vows but have written their own words which are special to them. Leo, would you like to speak first?'

Leo turned Violet to face him, taking both of her hands in his. 'My darling Violet,' he said, stunned at how choked up he was. He had to clear his throat before going on.

'Thank you for loving me…and for consenting to be my wife. I promise to be a faithful husband and to do everything in my power to bring you happiness. Everything I have is yours, my beautiful bride,' he said as he took the wedding band from Henry and slipped it on Violet's finger. 'My worldly goods. My body. And my unconditional love.'

Violet knew it was her turn then, but she found she could not speak at first. It didn't help that her mother had started weeping. But when Leo gave her fingers a gentle squeeze she gathered herself and took Leo's wedding band from his father.

'My darling Leo,' she said. 'Thank you for loving me and for asking me to marry you. I promise to be a faithful wife and do everything in my power to bring you happiness. You are my hero, my one true love. I will care for you and cherish you all the days of my life.' So saying, she slipped the wedding band on his finger.

Leo saw the moisture pooling in her eyes in tandem with his own. Thankfully the celebrant, perhaps sensing that emotion was in full flow and about to break banks, pronounced them man and wife without further ado.

Leo didn't wait for permission to kiss the bride, sweeping Violet into his arms straight away. And it was whilst they were kissing that the nine o'clock fireworks started, a welcome distraction for the others and for the rather emotional couple.

'I love you, Violet,' Leo murmured against her trembling mouth, his arms tightening around her.

'Do you think we could leave now?' Violet whispered back.

'I don't think so. Not yet, anyway.'

'Oh. Pity.'

'Weddings aren't just for the happy couple, you know. They're also for their families. At least that was what you told me.'

'Silly me.'

'No, not silly at all. Sweet. Besides, there's no hurry, is there? We have the rest of our lives together.'

'Oh,' Violet said with the happiest of sighs. 'I *do* like the sound of that.'

* * * * *

Mills & Boon® Large Print

August 2013

MASTER OF HER VIRTUE
Miranda Lee

THE COST OF HER INNOCENCE
Jacqueline Baird

A TASTE OF THE FORBIDDEN
Carole Mortimer

COUNT VALIERI'S PRISONER
Sara Craven

THE MERCILESS TRAVIS WILDE
Sandra Marton

A GAME WITH ONE WINNER
Lynn Raye Harris

HEIR TO A DESERT LEGACY
Maisey Yates

SPARKS FLY WITH THE BILLIONAIRE
Marion Lennox

A DADDY FOR HER SONS
Raye Morgan

ALONG CAME TWINS...
Rebecca Winters

AN ACCIDENTAL FAMILY
Ami Weaver

Mills & Boon® Large Print

September 2013

A RICH MAN'S WHIM
Lynne Graham

A PRICE WORTH PAYING?
Trish Morey

A TOUCH OF NOTORIETY
Carole Mortimer

THE SECRET CASELLA BABY
Cathy Williams

MAID FOR MONTERO
Kim Lawrence

CAPTIVE IN HIS CASTLE
Chantelle Shaw

HEIR TO A DARK INHERITANCE
Maisey Yates

ANYTHING BUT VANILLA...
Liz Fielding

A FATHER FOR HER TRIPLETS
Susan Meier

SECOND CHANCE WITH THE REBEL
Cara Colter

FIRST COMES BABY...
Michelle Douglas